"Don't you th
stop pretendi
each other?" Dal said.

"I'm sorry, Dal. I...I didn't know what to say. I just didn't think it mattered anymore."

"Well, it does. And I've still got some questions you may not want to answer."

Julie's mind raced as those old feelings of dread and fear seeped through every pore in her body. "Like what?"

"Like why you stopped writing me. And why you wouldn't return my phone calls. What happened, Julie? You just disappeared off the face of the earth. Why did you abandon me?"

Her gaze locked with his. In his eyes, she saw all the anguish she'd caused him. All the pain she herself felt inside. "I never meant to hurt you, Dal. Please believe I didn't have a choice. Not really."

"No choice?" His voice escalated, betraying his anger. "You stopped all communication with me. Without any justification at all. Why?"

"I had my reasons. That's all I can say."

How could she tell him the truth?

Books by Leigh Bale

Love Inspired

The Healing Place
The Forever Family
The Road to Forgiveness
The Forest Ranger's Promise
The Forest Ranger's Husband
The Forest Ranger's Child
Falling for the Forest Ranger
Healing the Forest Ranger
The Forest Ranger's Return

LEIGH BALE

is an award-winning, multi-published novelist who won the prestigious RWA Golden Heart in 2006. More recently, she was a finalist for the Gayle Wilson Award of Excellence. She is the daughter of a retired U.S. forest ranger, holds a B.A. in History with honors and loves grandkids, spending time with family, weeding the garden with her dog Sophie, and watching the little sagebrush lizards that live in her rock flowerbeds.

Married in 1981 to the love of her life, Leigh and her professor husband now have two wonderful children and two grandchildren. But life has not always been rosy. In 1996, Leigh's seven-year-old daughter was diagnosed with an inoperable brain tumor. In the dark years that followed, God never abandoned them. After six surgeries, two hundred and eighty-four stitches, a year of chemo, and a myriad of other difficulties, Leigh's daughter is now a grown woman and considered less than one percent survivorship in the world for her type of tumor. Life is good!

Truly the Lord has blessed Leigh's family. She now transfers the love and faith she's known into the characters of her stories. Readers who have their own trials can find respite within the uplifting message of Leigh's books. You can reach Leigh at P.O. Box 61381, Reno, Nevada 89506, or visit her website at www.leighbale.com.

The Forest Ranger's Return

Leigh Bale

HARLEQUIN® LOVE INSPIRED®

™ LOVE INSPIRED BOOKS

ISBN-13: 978-0-373-04276-0

THE FOREST RANGER'S RETURN

This edition published by arrangement with Love Inspired Books.

www.Harlequin.com

Printed in U.S.A.

For the Son of man
is not come to destroy men's lives, but to save them.
—*Luke* 9:56

This book is dedicated to my Aunt Joan.
Boy, do I ever love you, babe!

And thanks again to Sara Goldberg, a prosthetist with Hanger Clinic. This is the second book where your knowledge and expertise has helped me immensely.

Also, many thanks to Barbara Chastain (Center for Adaptive Riding, Reno, Nevada), Carrie Davis (Empowering Amputees), Alyssa Gale (Camp Riley), Edward Hicks (Adventure Camp), Chris Platt, and Beverly Skaggs (Hanger Clinic). Each of these wonderful people provided me with details big and small on how to run a camp for amputee kids and how to deal with a prosthesis. The world is a much better place because we have folks like you.

I apologize profusely for any errors in this book. They are mine alone.

Chapter One

Dallin Savatch breathed deep of the cool morning air. Stepping off the wraparound porch at Sunrise Ranch, he glanced at the damp dirt road surrounded by fields of newly sprouting alfalfa. Dark shadows clung to the jagged peaks of the McClellan Mountains, a hint of sunlight brightening the eastern sky. All was quiet; no one else was up yet. A whispering breeze carried the tangy scent of sage, horses and rain. Though the May weather had been unseasonably warm, a spring storm had struck in the middle of the night, awakening Dal with a clap of thunder. His left leg ached and he wasn't able to get back to sleep.

Phantom pain, his doctor called it.

That didn't prevent him from taking his morning run. Even at age thirty-six, nothing kept him from exercising his legs. He feared the wheelchair and losing his independence too much. Feared becoming less of a man than he already was.

He walked across the graveled driveway, then leaned against the hitching rail next to the barn. Wrapping his fingers around the coarse wood, he stretched his body for several minutes. The exercise warmed up his stiff muscles and relaxed the tight tendons.

Magpie, a gentle gray mare who didn't mind little kids tugging on her mane, stood inside the corral. She lifted her head over the rail fence and snuffled at him.

"Sorry, girl. No sugar cubes this early in the morning." Dal rubbed her between the ears. Then he turned and jogged toward the main road, picking up speed as he headed toward town, five miles away. He settled into an easy rhythm, his body moving well. Arms pumping. Blood pounding against his temples. Inhaling oxygen into his lungs.

He got his second wind just as he passed the turnoff to Secret Valley. His first-mile marker, where the graveled road turned into asphalt. His breathing came in even exhales. He was moving strong. Feeling invincible. But he knew from experience that was an illusion. Life was fragile, the human body easily broken.

He reached the main road, the sole of his running shoe pounding against the pavement. Another two miles and he'd turn back toward home. A rivulet of sweat tickled between his shoulder blades. He liked this quiet time when he jogged six miles before most people even started their day. He liked being alone to think about the work he had ahead of him back at the ranch. Horses to feed, stalls to muck out, bridles to repair, wild mustangs to train. Running not only cleared his head but also kept him in excellent condition. Something he valued more than anything else, except his relationship with God.

His gaze skimmed the fertile fields. A thin creek wound its lazy path through the valley and widened as it ran parallel to the road. Not once had he regretted his decision to move to Stokely, Nevada, the small ranching town where Cade Baldwin, his best friend, had settled and started a family of his own. Though Dal frequently felt like an intruder, the Baldwins were the closest thing to a family he would ever have, and he loved them dearly.

He focused on the terrain in front of him. Through the thick cluster of cattails, he caught a glimpse of Black Angus cattle nestled among the green pasture, chewing their cud. Soon they'd be up foraging for grass.

And then he spied a woman. Running toward him through the field on the opposite side of the stream. Through the tall willows, he could just make out the top half of her white jogging shirt and blue shorts. She pumped her bare arms hard as she ran. Sunlight gleamed against her long chestnut ponytail. Even from this distance, Dal caught the unwavering glint in her eyes. The lock-jawed determination to push herself hard.

Obviously a morning runner like him.

She glanced his way and waved. He lifted his hand in a halfhearted acknowledgment. Ever since he'd returned from the war in Afghanistan, he'd avoided women. His fiancée had broken off their engagement, and he couldn't really blame her. He no longer had much to offer a woman.

"Oww!" The stranger crumpled to the ground, disappearing from view.

Dal's mouth dropped open in surprise. She'd gone down! Maybe needed his help.

Leaving the road, he stepped down the graveled incline. He found a narrow spot in the creek where he could cross without wading through the muddy water. Gripping branches of willows, he pulled himself up the embankment. As he trotted toward the spot where he'd seen her fall, he called out, "You okay, ma'am?"

A thin wail came from the tall meadow grass. He found her lying on her side as she clutched her right ankle tight against her chest. She clenched her eyes closed and bit her bottom lip, fighting off a spasm of pain.

"Hey, you all right?" He stooped over her,

giving her time to catch her breath. Hoping it wasn't serious.

She jerked her head around and gasped in surprise. "You… You're…"

She didn't finish her sentence, her gaze lowering to his legs. She sucked in a harsh breath, no doubt caught off guard by his prosthesis and the absence of his left leg. He got this a lot, though he never got used to it. It was an automatic response for people to stare at his legs, but he hated it with every fiber of his being.

Correction. One leg. He was an amputee above his left knee. This morning, he wore his black J-shaped running prosthesis made out of flexible carbon fibers. He wore a regular C-Leg prosthesis for walking, but he loved and wore the J-Leg whenever he could. To the point that his handicap was no longer a handicap. Not if you considered the two gold medals he'd won in the Paralympics years earlier.

He braced himself as her gaze surfed past his running shorts to his good leg, a long, muscular limb dusted by a smattering of dark hair. He ignored her wince of sympathy.

"I… Yes, I'm fine. The pain is subsiding," she said.

As she pushed herself into a sitting position, he studied her face. Something familiar about her tugged at his memory. The tilt of her head. The shape of her chin and the warm, golden color of her eyes.

And then recognition struck him like a jolt of electricity. In spite of the two decades that had passed, he knew her.

Julie Granger.

A man just didn't forget the first girl he ever kissed.

She made a pretense of brushing dirt off her arms and knees. Staring at the ground. Staring at the trees. Staring anywhere but at him.

Didn't she recognize him, too? Maybe she was so distracted by his legs that she hadn't taken a good enough look at his face.

After all these years, he should be used to this by now. But he wasn't. Though he felt grateful to be able to walk and run again, the war had taken almost everything from him.

His leg. His fiancée. And almost his self-respect.

She peeled back the cuff of her white sock and rubbed her ankle. The movement commanded his gaze. Nice, trim ankles and shapely calves. He was still a man after all, and could appreciate a pair of pretty legs.

"May I?" He reached out a hand and she nodded.

He pressed his fingers gently against her bones, testing the structure for damage. Bloody abrasions scuffed her smooth skin, but he didn't have access to a first-aid kit right then. A battery of questions bludgeoned his mind. Where had she been all these years? How had life treated her? Was she married with a passel of kids? And why had she abandoned him so long ago?

"Nothing broken. You've probably just got a nasty sprain," he said.

Bracing her hands behind her, she leaned back and looked at him with a mix of dread and amazement. But not a smidgeon of recognition.

His heart rate ratcheted up several notches, and he felt suddenly protective of her. Just like the night her parents were killed. Only now he wasn't a young, powerless kid who couldn't stop Social Services from taking her away.

She shook her head with disgust. "This was so stupid of me. I took my eyes off my path and stepped in that hole over there."

She pointed at a rather deep gopher hole camouflaged by clumps of bleached grass.

"It's probably not good to run in the fields. They're very bumpy and hard on the legs," he said.

He wanted to tell her who he was, but something held him back. Something he didn't understand. Of all the people in the world, he hated for Julie to see him like this. One legged. No longer whole. But she'd turned her back on him long ago, and his situation would probably be of little importance to her now.

"How'd you lose your leg?" she asked.

He blinked, taken aback by her blunt question. But Julie had always been like that. Never mean or cruel. She'd just spoken her mind. At least until she'd disappeared from his life.

As if realizing her mistake, her face flushed. "I'm sorry. That was rude. It's none of my business."

"No, it's okay. Most people pretend they don't notice my missing leg. I lost it in Afghanistan." But her candor still surprised him. A lot. And very few people surprised him these days.

"You're in the military?" She sat forward again, looking interested.

"Not anymore. I'm a marine." He tightened his mouth, not wanting to disclose too much about himself. To anyone. Especially a girl he'd loved when he was fifteen years old and too young to know anything about the world.

"Ah, well, thank you for your service to our country. And I'm so sorry for your loss."

He caught the tone of sincerity in her soft voice. No pity, just gratitude.

She braced herself to stand, and he reached out an arm. "Here, let me help you."

She eyed him, looking skeptical. Then, without a word, she accepted his offer, sliding her fingers against his.

Trusting him.

The warmth of her soft skin zinged through his arm. He tightened his grip and pulled her up, then let her go and stepped back.

"You think you can walk? Or should I call someone for you? A husband, maybe…?"

"No, I've never been married," she said.

Alone, just like him.

Surely he imagined the subtle throb of regret in her voice. And yet, a single man of his age was probably more sensitive to other people in the same predicament. But he was still amazed that she didn't seem to remember him.

"I'll get my truck and drive you home," he offered.

She glanced at his amputated leg again, as though assessing his abilities. He knew what she was thinking. They were out in the middle of nowhere. How could he get his truck and drive her home with only one leg?

He jabbed a thumb toward the vicinity of Sunrise Ranch, which was now shrouded behind an edge of mountains. "I don't live far from here. You'd only have to wait a few minutes."

His gaze skimmed past the white stripe along her blue runner's shorts to her scratched knees. A streak of dirt marred the edge of her chin, and he longed to brush it away. To touch her and make sure she was real. He hated being perceived as weak, especially by a girl from his past.

Correction. Woman. She wasn't a child anymore. And neither was he.

"Um, no. I don't think that'll be necessary. I can walk home."

She applied slight pressure to her ankle, testing to see if it could bear her weight. As she took a few limping steps, her face immediately contorted with pain. He knew she couldn't walk home. Not like this.

"It's three miles into town. You're gonna

have to let me help you. Don't worry, it's what I do." He forced a smile.

Her beautiful eyes locked with his, filled with doubt. "What do you do?"

"I help people. I always have." But he hadn't been able to help her twenty years ago. In so many words, he'd asked her to trust him. Again. And yet, he'd failed her once. He'd been too young to stop her from being taken away. To protect her from being hurt by people she didn't even know. But now he was a grown man. Things were different. Being a protector was in his blood. It was what had driven him to become a U.S. Marine. What had driven him to save Cade Baldwin's life in Afghanistan. And what drove him now to train horses and work with amputee kids.

Because they needed him. And it felt good to be needed.

"Okay, thank you." And then she smiled. A stunning reminder of who she was. The expression lit up her entire face, curved her generous lips and crinkled the slim bridge of her nose. If he'd had any doubts before, he lost them now. This was Julie Granger.

His first love.

He took a deep breath, then thrust his hand out in greeting. "I'm Dallin Savatch. Most people call me Dal."

He watched her face carefully, waiting for recognition to fill her eyes. Nothing. Not even a glimmer.

Instead, she dragged her gaze down to his fingers. As though hesitant to touch him. He waited for her shiver of disgust. He'd seen it before, time and time again, with other people who couldn't get past his missing leg. But that shiver didn't come. Not this time.

She clasped his fingers tight and shook his hand. "My name is Julie Granger. I'm sorry to inconvenience you like this, but I really appreciate it."

So. She didn't know him. And he couldn't decide if that was good or bad. How could she forget him so easily? Was her memory lapse selective or real?

He decided to let it pass. To pretend he hadn't been hurt when she'd stopped answering his letters and returning his phone calls. He'd tried to tell himself she'd been nothing more than a high school crush, but that never stuck. He'd loved her deeply, but she no longer felt the same.

"No problem." He let go a bit too fast. Trying to put some distance between them. Trying not to feel angry by her presence. He wished she weren't so lovely. A woman who obviously liked running as much as he did. If that were possible.

"Why don't you sit over here while I hurry home and get my truck? Then I can drive you into town to Cade's office." He pointed at a soft grassy knoll at the side of the road beneath the spreading limbs of a tall cottonwood.

"Cade?" Her knees visibly wobbled as she took a step toward the inviting spot. He reached for her arm, and she didn't refuse.

"Cade Baldwin. My partner. He's the doctor in town."

"A doctor won't be necessary," she said. "Are you a doctor, too?"

"No, no. Cade's the doctor. We were in

the Marine Corps together. Now we're partners out at Sunrise Ranch. We pooled our resources and work together there. I mostly just handle the horses."

He'd always been a horseman, even when they were kids and his widowed mom had worked as a cook on a ranch in Oklahoma.

He expected Julie's doubtful stare directed toward his prosthesis, but she didn't even flinch. Most amputees didn't train horses, much less wild mustangs. But he did. And he was good at it, too. He refused to let his missing limb get in the way of his work. The horses didn't judge him. They didn't care if he only had one leg. And when he was with them, he could forget the disability he'd worked so hard to overcome.

The way Julie had forgotten him.

One of her brows arched upward in recognition. "Ah! You're from the horse camp for amputee kids I've been hearing about. I believe the previous forest ranger married the owner."

He nodded, surprised that she knew so much about them. "That's right. In fact, the horse camp was the ranger's idea. Cade's in charge of physical therapy and special programs for the kids. His wife, Lyn, pays the bills, coordinates the meals, takes care of her two children and everything else. Of course, we have other staff who work at the place, too."

"It sounds amazing," she agreed. "I've heard a lot about Lyn Baldwin since I got into town. I'm not surprised she retired as the forest ranger once she had her second child. No doubt she has plenty to keep her busy out at your ranch."

"She is amazing, but why have you heard about her?"

"I'm the new forest ranger."

Dawning flooded Dal's dazed brain. Lyn had told him a new ranger was coming in last week, but he'd expected a man, not Julie. Not a girl he'd never forgotten in all these long, painful years.

"I just moved here last week," she continued. "I'm hoping to visit Lyn soon, to see if she can bring me up to speed on several issues I'll be dealing with."

He nodded and released her hand as she sat down. Currents of energy zigzagged up his arm, reaching clear to his shoulder blade. He rubbed his biceps, hoping the feeling would ease soon.

It didn't.

"I'm sure Lyn would be glad to help you out," he said. "Just give her a call. Now, you wait right here and I'll go get my truck."

Without another word, he whirled around and dashed away, moving swiftly over the dirt road. Eager to get away from Julie's observant gaze.

He ran with no limp whatsoever. An amazing task, considering the rocky surface he'd chosen to jog on. But he'd gotten used to it, navigating the uneven fields and even hiking in the mountains like a man with two normal legs. He had a prosthesis for almost every activity, and that made his way of life possible.

And in that moment, Dal wished things could be different somehow. He'd paid a high price to save Cade's life in Afghanistan, and he'd gladly pay it again. He just wished he could have kept both his legs in the process. But Dal had long ago reconciled himself to the fact that life would never be the same. Not for him and Julie. Not ever again.

Julie stared at the tall man's broad shoulders as he hopped across the stream and returned to the main road. Her breath stuttered as she watched him move as gracefully as a man with two solid legs. If she hadn't seen it with her own eyes, she never would have believed Dal Savatch was an amputee.

She never should have decided to jog in the grassy fields, but she'd wanted to see what kinds of vegetation grew along the creek bed. To see what kinds of fish swam in the stream. And to assess if the area was being overgrazed. As the new forest ranger, it was her job.

She'd been concentrating on her task when she'd looked up at the road paralleling the creek and seen the most handsome man running toward her. Through the thick branches of willows, she'd caught glimpses of his rugged face. The blunt shape of his jaw. The determined lines carved around his mouth. The muscular torso and strong arms moving with his fast stride.

Dal Savatch. The love of her life. Or, at least, that was what she'd thought when she was fifteen. Before her parents had been killed in a horrible car crash. Before she'd been yanked out of her home and slapped into foster care.

When the vegetation had given way, she'd seen Dal's legs. The curving prosthesis he wore where his left leg should have been. An amputee, running smooth and fast along a dirt road that even challenged Julie's experienced stride.

Before she could catch herself, she'd stepped in a hole and gone down. Road rash never hurt as much as it did when someone else witnessed your fall. Her shocked attention had been on the man, not the rough terrain in front of her. Now she felt like a fool. She had twisted her ankle hard and she blinked to clear the sudden tears of pain, highly aware of the man who'd crossed the stream and come to her rescue.

Oh, Dal. What he must have suffered in losing his leg. It hurt her to see him like this. To think of the pain he must have gone through. She wasn't surprised he'd overcome such adversity. Dal never was a quitter. Never gave up on anything he wanted.

Never stopped writing or calling her, until she'd moved so often his letters could no longer find her.

Julie groaned, conscious of the rings of sweat on her jogging shirt. Reaching up, she patted her damp hair and regretted not putting on any makeup that morning. Dal had just gotten a good look at her, but he didn't recognize her. Didn't remember the sweet kiss they'd shared on the front porch of her childhood home the very night her parents had died.

Oh, well. Maybe it was for the best. At the age of thirty-five, Julie had long ago given up on marriage and family. She was what her last foster mom had called an old maid. But she couldn't help that she loved her career and liked being alone.

Most of the time.

Having lost her parents, she'd decided not to regret what she'd never really known. And yet, there were times when she'd seen other women in the grocery store, pushing their kids around in shopping carts. Hugging their husbands. Their laughter ringing through the air. And then a pang of regret would rip through Julie's heart, reminding her of what she'd never have for her very own.

A family. Someone who loved and needed her. Someone who cared if she lived or died.

She settled her back against the strong tree trunk and waited for Dal. The throbbing in her ankle had eased by the time the sound of an engine filled the air. She wrenched her head around. An old blue pickup truck rumbled down the dirt road, heading toward her. Dal sat in the driver's seat wearing a battered cowboy hat. He looked her way, a worried frown tugging at his handsome mouth and brows.

Worried for her?

He pulled the truck over and stepped out. A graceful movement that left her impressed by his mastery of the prosthesis. An embarrassing reminder that she was the one needing his assistance, not the other way around.

He rushed over to help her stand. Glancing up, her gaze locked with his. His features hadn't changed much since they were kids, but he'd grown taller and filled out in the shoulders, chest and arms.

As she stared into his hazel eyes, several pounding moments followed when he let down his guard. And in those few seconds, she read a lot in those brown-green depths. She saw the hurt he kept locked inside. The solemn sadness. The uncertainty. But no recognition. Then his eyes clouded over. A guarded look that told her he'd do the right thing no matter what, but he was scared.

Of her.

A foolish notion, surely. She was imagining things.

As he helped her hobble over to the passenger side of his truck, she tried not to lean against his solid warmth. Tried not to add any extra burden to his missing leg.

"I'm strong. You can lean on me." He spoke low, his gentle tone encouraging her to trust him.

She almost breathed a huge sigh of relief. For so long, she'd depended on no one but herself. She'd wanted to stay close to Dal, but with her orphaned status, her life had spiraled out of her control. Their separation was for the best.

She should act normal around this anything-but-normal man. After all, she didn't know him anymore. They were basically strangers. But in her mind, she couldn't help thinking that she'd never met another man like him, with or without legs.

Pulling the door open, he helped her inside and waited patiently while she snapped on her seat belt. Her skin still tingled where he'd touched her arms.

His gaze lowered to her ankle and his expression softened. "It doesn't look too swollen."

"No, it'll be fine." And she knew the

words were true. If Dal could recover from losing a leg, then she could surely survive a wrenched ankle.

He closed the door and went around to the driver's side. The cab of the truck smelled of peppermint. An old vehicle with a leather bench seat. A classic truck that must be at least fifty years old. She couldn't help wondering about his life and the man he'd become. Did he still like pistachio ice cream? Was he still a whiz at calculus? Was he married with kids of his own?

She longed to ask, but didn't dare. Guilt nibbled at her conscience for the anguish she must have caused when she'd stopped writing to him. It was better to forget.

She watched with detached interest as he got in and started the engine. He shifted the gears and drove slow and steady over the dirt road leading into town.

"Nice truck," she said.

"Thanks."

"What year?"

"Nineteen-sixty. I rebuilt the engine myself. It's therapeutic."

"I really appreciate your help," she said, feeling out of place. Feeling as if she should remind him of who she was. But what good would that do? Chatting about a past she'd rather forget wouldn't be much fun. Above all else, she didn't want his pity. She just wanted to forget what she'd been through.

"How long have you been running?" he asked, staring straight ahead as he used his right foot to press the gas and brake pedals, as needed.

"Since I was fifteen, when my parents died and I went into foster care." She hadn't meant to give him such a big reminder. The words had just slipped out before she could call them back. But this disconcerting man had caught her off guard. She couldn't help wondering if the clues would remind him of who she was. She didn't want to talk about her life, a habit she'd acquired over the years to protect herself from being hurt again. With good reason.

"I'm sorry to hear that," he said.

"How about you? When did you start running?"

"I guess I've always been a runner," he said. "First in high school when I played football and ran track, then as a marine. When I returned from the war, I ran to rehabilitate myself. To keep myself independent and out of a wheelchair." He clamped his mouth shut, as though he also regretted confiding so much.

Obviously she wasn't the only one with a painful past.

"I can understand your desire for independence," she said. "I heard about a 5K race they're holding here in the valley the latter part of August and thought I'd participate, as long as my ankle doesn't stop me. A race motivates me to get up early and run every morning. It also keeps me in shape in case I'm called out on a wildfire this summer."

He glanced her way, his brown-green eyes skimming over her bare calves and running shoes. "Yeah, I've already entered that race myself."

"Is that right? I can't say I'm surprised." Tilting her head, she chuckled. They still had things in common, but the reasons *why* they both ran intrigued her more than the running itself. Because, truth be told, Julie ran for the isolation of it. The solitude and healing. She'd been by herself so long that she didn't know anything else. And she'd never met a person she thought might fully understand her deeply buried motives.

Until now.

"Who are you running for?" she asked.

Or from? That was what she really wanted to know.

He tilted his head in question. "What do you mean?"

"Who's your sponsor?"

"Ah! Sunrise Ranch, of course. The amputee kids."

"Of course."

"And who's your sponsor?" he asked.

She shrugged. "I don't have one yet. I could use the Forest Service, but that might be viewed as a conflict of interest."

"Why?"

"Some people might not like the idea of a government agency sponsoring the new forest ranger. Some folks get touchy about things like that."

"Well, they shouldn't."

"I agree."

Within minutes, he pulled into the driveway of her white Forest Service house, located two blocks north of Main Street. From what her new range assistant had told her, Lyn Baldwin had lived here with her amputee daughter until she'd married Cade Baldwin and moved out to Sunrise Ranch.

Julie hadn't needed to give Dal directions to her house. Not surprising in such a small town. Throughout her career, she'd been transferred quite a bit and had worked hard for this promotion as a forest ranger. Now she hoped to put down roots. She might never be a wife and mother, but that didn't mean she couldn't become involved in her community.

A town that included Dal Savatch.

As he helped her amble up the path to her front porch, she noticed that the pain in her ankle was almost gone. Thank goodness. She had a full day of work ahead of her.

With starting a brand-new job, she didn't need a throbbing ankle to keep her from perusing all the timber and watershed reports sitting on her desk.

Dal took her key from her hand and inserted it in the lock. He opened the door, pushing it wide. He didn't come inside, but hesitated until she turned to face him. And then she realized that several minutes had passed in which she'd forgotten he was an amputee. She'd been so engrossed in her own discomfort that she hadn't noticed how he'd helped her up the front steps. Somehow, this man made her forget he was handicapped.

A flood of memories from her childhood surged through her mind. Dal pushing her on the tire swing in her backyard. Helping her move sprinkler pipes in her father's cornfield. Sitting with his arm around her shoulders as they rode the school bus each morning. In her mind, she couldn't think of him as anything but confident, whole and in control.

"You gonna be okay?" he asked.

"Yes, thanks for everything. I really appreciate it."

He lifted one strong hand and rested it against the threshold, his brows crinkled with thought. "Maybe once your leg is feeling better, we could run together. In the mornings. To prepare for the race. It might be safer if you have a running partner."

His face flushed and he stepped back. She realized that he was embarrassed by the offer. Maybe he even regretted it.

She hesitated, liking this idea. And why not? Dal Savatch was nice enough. She didn't have any friends in town. Not yet. Maybe spending time with this man from her past might help alleviate the hollow loneliness that had taken up residence within her heart.

"I'd like that very much," she said.

Then she thought better of it. Dal Savatch was too likable. Too easy to talk to. Renewing their relationship could backfire on her. And then what?

"I'll see you later." He hurried down the steps, as though he wanted to escape.

Before she could change her mind.

As he strode gracefully back to his truck, she stared at his wide shoulders. No second thoughts. Not now.

Without another word, she went inside and closed the door. An empty void settled inside her chest. As she hobbled down the hallway to her bedroom, she knew she'd be late getting in to work that morning. She also knew she'd see Dal Savatch again sometime soon. Perhaps tomorrow morning. Or the next. And somehow that was okay for now. It had taken years for her to process her grief. Her psychologist had taught her not to think about the past or worry about the future. And she wouldn't. Because she and Dal Savatch could never be anything more than friends.

Chapter Two

Julie didn't go running the next day. Or the next. Dal knew, because he watched for her. She must be home resting her ankle. But after three more days and no sign of her, he started to worry. He couldn't help himself. And he didn't like that. Because worrying led to caring, which led to heartbreak.

Julie Granger meant nothing to him. Just a blast from his past. He barely knew her, but that didn't seem to matter. After all this time, he couldn't get her off his mind. Her silent rejection from years past still haunted him.

A week later, he couldn't wait any longer. He pulled his old truck into a parking place next to the McClellan National Forest Service office. After killing the engine, he slid the keys from the ignition and thrust the door wide-open. He slipped the keys into one pocket of his faded blue jeans, then swiveled around in his seat, placed both his booted feet on the ground, braced his hands against the frame of the door, got his balance and stood. A swift series of motions no one seemed to notice. But for Dal, each action required concentration if he didn't want to fall flat on his face.

Rotating his left hip forward, he stepped up from the curb. With not a hint of a limp, he walked past the American flag waving in the breeze. Morning sunlight rested on the red tulips and yellow daffodils blooming in the flowerbeds that lined the redbrick building. Within moments, he reached the double glass doors, pushed them open and stood inside the reception room. The aroma of coffee filtered through the air, along with the click of someone typing on a keyboard and a phone ringing down the hall.

He hesitated, thinking he shouldn't be here. Thinking he should have insisted that Cade come instead. But the truth was, Dal wanted to see Julie again. To find out if her ankle had healed. To go jogging with her.

To catch up on her life.

He tried to tell himself this visit was all about business. To develop a horse trail and campsite for amputee kids out at Sunrise Ranch. And yet, he knew it was something more. Something he didn't understand.

He also knew that being near Julie might put him on a one-way collision course to heartache. He could never fall in love again. Never marry. Never have a family of his own. The secret he kept hidden deep inside his soul wouldn't allow him to pretend.

So why was he here?

He still wasn't quite sure. And that thought caused him to turn and reach for the door handle. Ready to leave. Ready to run away.

"Hi, Dal. Can I help you?" Shauna Cline, the receptionist, greeted him. A woman of perhaps fifty years, her red cheeks plumped with her smile.

He nodded politely. "Hi, Shauna. I… I'm here to see the new forest ranger, if she's available."

"Do you have an appointment?"

Dal shook his head. "Nope, sorry."

He'd never needed an appointment to visit Lyn Baldwin when she'd been the forest ranger here. But after marrying Dal's best friend and having two children, Lyn had retired to become a full-time mom six months earlier. Maybe Julie was a bit stuffier, but he doubted it. Not from what he remembered about her. Julie Granger had always been laid-back and easygoing. Anything but conventional.

But that was before her folks had died. She could have changed. Life had a funny way of doing that to people.

"Excuse me one moment, and I'll see if she's free." Shauna stepped around the counter and bustled down the hall.

Glancing at the clock on the wall, Dal noted the time. He thumbed through a pamphlet on preventing forest fires. He didn't sit down, and he didn't have to wait long.

"Dal! This is a pleasant surprise." Julie greeted him with a tight smile and stiff shoulders. In her eyes, he saw a hesitancy that told him his visit was anything but pleasing to her.

"How's your ankle?" Dal shook her hand, his gaze swishing over her spruce-green pants and the bronze shield pinned just above the left front pocket of her drab olive-color Forest Service shirt. A drastic change from the running shorts and shoes she'd been wearing last week. The uniform seemed odd to Dal. He had to remind himself that she was a professional woman, and the tables had turned on him. He now needed her help.

"Fine. I just started running again yesterday morning."

And he'd missed her somehow. Maybe that was a good thing.

"I'm glad to hear it." He glanced at Shauna, who sat at her desk watching them with attentive gray eyes. "Um, I'm here in an official capacity. I have a business proposal I'd like to discuss, if you have the time."

"Sure! Come on back." She spun around and headed down the hallway, glancing over her shoulder to make sure he followed.

He did, trying not to stare at the gentle swing of her hips. He couldn't get over the graceful change in her. What a shame life had cheated them out of growing up together, going to college and possibly marrying. If her parents hadn't died, he might not have gone to war. He wouldn't have been there to save Cade Baldwin's life, and he wouldn't have lost his leg.

What kind of man might he have become if Julie hadn't been yanked out of his life? It did no good to think about it, but he couldn't help wondering.

Her office wasn't overly large, but included an alcove where a wide mahogany conference table sat surrounded by six tall-backed chairs. Stacks of reports rested in tidy piles along the edge of her desk. He gazed at a picture of two desert bighorn sheep hanging on one wall and a mule deer standing beside a mountain stream on the other. She obviously still loved the outdoors, just as he did.

She rounded the desk. "Please, have a seat."

He sat opposite her, conscious of her watching him. Glad the desk provided a barrier between them.

"So what can I do for you?" Her chair creaked as she sat back and crossed her legs.

He cleared his throat. "There's an old mountain trail just south of Sunrise Ranch. It comes out on the other side along Lake McClellan. I don't know of many people who use it except me. We'd like to develop the trail a bit more and even put a campsite at the top of the mountain where it overlooks the lake."

"You want to alter a trail that already exists?" she clarified.

He nodded, wishing he'd asked Cade to come and make this request instead. He longed to blurt out the truth to Julie. That he knew her, had never forgotten her and wished he could tell her his darkest, most hurtful secret of all. "Yes, we want to take some of our amputee kids up there on horses for an overnight camping experience."

Without a word, she stood and reached for a round canister sitting behind the door. Opening it, she unrolled a large map of the area and spread it across the conference table. She waved for him to join her. "Can you show me exactly where the trail is located?"

He stood and walked to her side. Her gaze dipped to his legs, but he knew she saw nothing of his prosthesis beneath the cover of his blue jeans and scuffed cowboy boots.

She bent over the table, her hands smoothing the map before she pointed at a small red star. "This is where we are in town." She skimmed her index finger over the map toward the east. "And this is Sunrise Ranch. Here's Lake McClellan. Where's this trail you want to develop?"

He leaned closer to inspect the map. Bold green numbers indicated the locations of Forest Service trails and campsites in the area. A legend at the bottom of the map named each trail. He recognized several, but it took him a moment to find the isolated one he sought. He couldn't concentrate. The citrus fragrance of Julie's shampoo distracted him and he blinked several times, trying to focus.

"Right here." He traced a thin line rising over a mountain peak and skirting the northeastern side of the lake.

She peered at the spot. "Number eighteen. Gilway Trail."

"Gilway," he repeated.

"Probably the name of the person credited with finding the path." Without explanation, she stepped over to the wall and yanked open the drawer of a metal cabinet. Her long fingers skimmed the lips of manila folders before she pulled one file out and laid it open on the table. A rustle of papers followed as she flipped through the pages, her eyes narrowing as she skimmed several paragraphs of various reports.

Dal watched in fascination, impressed by her obvious interest in the topic. Finally, she stood back and smiled wide.

"Gilway has been around for ages. No one

really knows when it originated. Probably used by the Indians as an old hunting trail before the white man even lived in this area. It's already zoned for hikers and pedestrians. Semiprimitive nonmotorized."

"Nonmotorized?"

"Yep. That means no snowmobiles, motorbikes, cars, trucks or engines of any kind. Except chain saws, of course. In case we need to fight a wildfire up there."

Good. He liked that. "What about horses?"

"Horses are okay."

A feeling of relief swept over him. He'd ridden that trail many times and didn't want to get in trouble for taking a horse up there.

"No campsite presently exists at the top," Julie continued. "Just the trail. As far as I can tell, it's been recently used by an occasional hunter and the Back Country Horsemen. Beautiful scenic views. Very close to your ranch. You've chosen wisely."

"Yeah, I knew the first time I went up there that it was a therapeutic place to take amputee kids."

"How often do you plan to use the trail and campsite?" she asked.

"Maybe seven nights total throughout the months of July and August, not including the times I ride up there on my own."

"And you just want a camping experience for the kids?"

"Yes, to help them build a feeling of independence and self-esteem. We have horseback riding for all the children back at the ranch, but only those kids who have some experience and confidence riding a horse will be allowed to go on the overnight campout. Above all else, we want to ensure their safety."

She leaned her hip against the edge of the table and folded her arms. "That's good. How many people will you have going up there at one time?"

"Maybe four or five kids and the same number of adults each time."

"With a horse for every person?"

He nodded. "And several pack horses, too."

"That sounds okay, but keep in mind that

crowding can reduce the quality of your experience up there. You won't want to overdo it."

"We'll keep that in mind. So what comes next?"

She stepped back from the table. "The first thing I need to do is take a ride with you to see the layout of the trail and find out if it's even possible for us to develop a campsite up there."

"A ride? With me?" His voice sounded a bit strained to his own ears. Did he look as nervous as he felt?

"Yes, if possible. Then you can show me exactly what you have in mind. I can take my Forest Service horse. Do you have a horse you can ride?"

His heart gave a funny leap of excitement. The thought of spending time up on the mountain with this interesting woman brought him a feeling of anticipation he couldn't deny. "Yeah, I can do that."

"Good. What if I drive out to your place with my horse next week on Friday morning, about nine o'clock? I suspect our work will take the better part of the day, so we should pack lunches and plenty of water."

"That sounds fine to me."

"After I've inspected the area, I'll need to perform an environmental assessment on the proposal."

"What's an environmental assessment?" he asked.

"It's where I look at the work we need to do in altering the trail. The potential for erosion, the possible impact on the public and wildlife, the impact if we alter any vegetation and the scenery. Stuff like that. Before we build a campsite, I'll need to also advertise this development in the newspaper and hold a public meeting for anyone who cares to attend."

He frowned, thinking this sounded logical, but worried about what it might mean for the project. "Do we have to hold an open meeting?"

"Yes, why?"

"Some local ranchers may not like this idea. They can be rather difficult at times."

She shrugged. "Then I'll listen to what

they have to say. It's my job to respond to any legitimate concerns people might have. At this point, I don't see any problems. But you never know what might crop up."

"How long will all of this take?"

"Normally the entire process takes about two years."

His heart plummeted. "I was hoping to get everything ready so we can use the campsite by next summer."

The corners of her mouth creased in a smile. The expression lit up her entire face and made her soft brown eyes sparkle. Wow, she was pretty.

"Since this is for such a good cause, I think we can expedite the process," she said.

A breath of relief filtered through his lungs. "Thanks, Julie. I appreciate your help. More than I can say."

She chuckled. "Thank me later, after I've performed the assessment and told you what we can and can't do."

He frowned. "Should I be worried?"

She waved a hand. "Not yet. Let's wait and see what we're working with. You can worry later, after we find out what it's going to cost. Then we'll have to decide how to get the work done."

He hadn't thought about expense. "I've got access to some manpower, but not a lot of funds."

"That's okay for now. I've got some ideas that should help us out in that area. Once I've completed the assessment, I'll need to issue you a special-use permit. No work can be done on the trail until then. And every phase of work will need to be inspected and approved. Understood?"

"Understood."

They spoke for several more minutes, confirming their meeting time and discussing the options. By the time Dal left Julie's office, he felt confident this trail and campsite would greatly augment the program they offered amputee kids at Sunrise Ranch. He also feared this was a huge mistake.

He couldn't help enjoying being near Julie again. Gone was the little girl he once knew, replaced by an educated, beautiful, confident woman. But escalating his involvement with the ranger might prove deadly to his heart. He'd do it anyway, starting with his morning run. Like a freight train running out of track, he couldn't stop now. Developing Gilway Trail would benefit the amputee kids, and jogging with Julie would help keep her safe. It would also give him an opportunity to find out about her life.

He just hoped he didn't regret it all later on.

Julie sat at her desk and jotted some notes to herself. Trying to focus on work. Trying to stop thinking about the man who had just left her office.

Her body trembled. Several times, she'd been ready to blurt out the truth. That she remembered Dal, the plans they'd made and the hopes they'd shared. But that had all been ruined by one of her foster dads. A horrible, smelly man who had stolen her innocence and trust.

Focus, Julie. Don't think about the past. Just move forward. You're safe now. You don't need anyone but yourself.

She tugged her thoughts back to her work. First thing, she should have Shauna draft an advertisement for an open meeting to put in the local newspaper. She could imagine some of the concerns the local people might have about Dal's proposed project, and she planned to prepare beforehand. There was plenty of time for that. She'd know more once she viewed the trail with Dal in a few days.

Next, she should begin a preliminary environmental assessment and consider the animals that might be impacted by this change. Desert bighorn sheep. Rocky Mountain mule deer. Canadian geese….

She stopped writing, her hands shaking. The pen dropped to the desk. She laced her fingers together in a tight grip. Resting her elbows on top of her yellow lined notepad, she leaned her forehead against her fists and exhaled a tight breath.

This is just work. Just a very nice, attractive man you used to know. No need to be upset. It's just business.

She tried to reason with herself. Tried to

calm the anxious feelings rumbling around inside her mind. She'd overcome so much in her past and thought she'd learned to deal with men one-on-one. But maybe not. For some reason, Dal Savatch touched on old memories she thought were long buried. He was one of the few men who had tried to protect her from being hurt, even if he had been merely a boy at the time. So why did his presence bother her so intensely?

She knew. She didn't need to ask herself the question. She liked him and longed to confide in him. She wanted to be friends with him again. Maybe more than friends. But she couldn't. Not now, not ever. So she was upset. Because of the shame and uncertainty of her past, she didn't know how he might take the truth of what had happened to her.

The fear.

Pushing her chair back, she stood and slid past her desk to stand in front of the only window in her office. She used her thumb and index finger to widen the slatted blinds and peered outside at the empty parking lot.

No sign of Dal's old pickup truck. Just her compact car and a few other vehicles that belonged to her staff members. Not a single person in sight.

Dal was fast, she'd give him that. And light on his feet. For the entire length of their meeting, she'd completely forgotten about his amputation. Until he'd left. And even then, she couldn't believe how easily he moved. Smooth, graceful and masculine. Like he had no impediment at all.

She had nothing to worry about. No need to feel distressed by his presence in her office. And if he finally remembered who she was, she could act surprised and brush it off. For now, she'd focus on her work, help develop the trail and campsite and nothing more. She didn't expect anything else, and neither did Dal.

Or did she?

That was just the problem. In spite of her reasoning and resolve, she wanted more. For the first time in twenty years, she wished…

No! She didn't need a man in her life. She didn't need anyone. She'd done just fine on her own. A solid education, a comfortable home and a challenging career. If she got close to Dal again, he'd want an explanation as to why she'd stopped writing and calling. Her reasons were her own, and she couldn't talk about them with him. It had taken a gargantuan effort just to discuss her sexual abuse with her psychologist. Telling an old boyfriend about it was impossible. Being by herself was for the best. No complications. No angst. No pain.

But maybe that was all wrong. Maybe she should put herself out there with Dal and see what life might bring her way. Maybe…

No! She whirled away from the window and returned to her desk. Plopping down into her chair, she picked up the pen, leaned over the desk and forced herself to write.

Vegetation impacts. Juniper. Aspen. Willows. Indian paintbrush. Snowberry….

She dropped the pen again and stared at the notepad. Moisture blurred the words in front of her eyes. She dashed the tears away, thinking she was being silly and emotional.

Jerking open the top drawer of her desk,

she gazed at a picture of her parents. She kept it close by so she could look at them any time she liked. So she wouldn't forget. But she didn't leave the picture sitting out on her desk. Not where other people might see and start asking personal questions.

Why did Dal have to reenter her life? Why now? Over the years, she'd coped with being on her own. She'd dealt with her insecurities and fears. Hadn't she?

Apparently not. At least not since Dallin Savatch had rushed back into her life.

She owed him an explanation. Her unexplained silence hadn't been fair to him. If he knew the truth, he'd understand. He'd forgive her. But she couldn't utter the words. Not now. Not ever.

Snapping the drawer closed, she reached for her purse. She had to get out of here. Had to clear her head.

Her fingers tightened around the straps as she slung the bag over her shoulder and stood. Gathering up a pile of files she'd set aside earlier, she walked to the door.

She was a mature, professional woman,

not a vulnerable little girl anymore. Dal Savatch needed her help. She could assist him and Sunrise Ranch. That was all. Other than offering to run with her in the mornings, Dal hadn't suggested anything more. He didn't even remember her. She was making too much out of this situation.

Wasn't she?

Walking down the hallway, she paused at Shauna's desk long enough to tell the woman she was going home. And tomorrow afternoon, she'd drive out to Sunrise Ranch and visit with Lyn Baldwin. She'd spoken to the former ranger a couple days earlier by phone, and Lyn had told her to stop by anytime. Julie wanted to discuss several projects Lyn had been working on during her time as ranger. Hopefully, Lyn could clarify a few things for Julie.

In the process, Julie also hoped she might gain more insight into Dal Savatch. What it was about the man that she still found so appealing. And why she feared becoming friends with him again. Maybe then Julie could finally reconcile herself with the past and get the man off her mind.

Then again, maybe not.

Chapter Three

At 5:33 the next morning, Julie flipped off the kitchen light and stepped out onto her front porch. Hazy sunlight filtered past her neighbors' dew-laden lawns. She breathed deep of the crisp air and shivered, wondering if she'd need a jacket for her daily jog. She decided no, that her exercise would soon make her hot and the breeze would cool her off.

Looking up, she froze.

Dal Savatch stood leaning against a tall cottonwood on the opposite side of her white picket fence. Dressed like her in runner's shoes and shorts, he rested his weight on his good leg. With his arms folded, his large biceps stretched his gray T-shirt tight. Even as a teenager, he'd been well built, with muscles any girl would admire. But the fully grown man he'd become almost made Julie drool.

As the screen door clapped closed behind her, he lifted his head. Even from this distance, she could feel his penetrating stare like a physical blow. Lowering his arms, he stepped away from the tree. He paused at the gate, not entering the perimeter of her yard, but waiting for her to come down the front steps and join him.

"It's a bit early for a visit. What are you doing here?" she asked, trying not to sound curt.

"Waiting for you. Remember, I promised to run with you."

"You don't need to do that, Dal. It's a long distance out of your way." Yes, she remembered his promise, but she hadn't expected him to keep it. Not really.

"I want to." He blinked, as though embarrassed by his admission.

He reached over and lifted the latch before pushing the gate open for her.

"Thanks." She stepped onto the sidewalk.

His gentlemanly manners reminded her of the conscientious boy he'd always been. When other boys had paid their girlfriends little mind, Dal had rushed ahead to open doors for her, had brought her yellow roses from his mother's flower garden, had said please and thank-you. In high school, Julie had been the envy of every other girl. Because she'd had Dal.

"So how long have you been waiting here?" She walked to the tree he'd vacated and braced her hands against the coarse trunk before stretching her calf muscles. Trying to appear unaffected by his presence.

"Not long," he said.

"You could have come inside the house."

"No, I didn't want to intrude until you were ready to go."

But what did he want? And why did his presence unnerve her so much?

"How far do you usually run?" She made small talk, avoiding the real questions pounding in her brain. Thank goodness he didn't remember her and their whispered promises to each other twenty years earlier. Part of her longed for him to recognize her. The part that still cared for him and wished he felt the same.

Puppy love, her mom had called it before she'd died. But Julie had never felt anything so real before or since.

"I usually run six miles. And you?" Taking a position on the opposite side of the tree, he braced his left hand against the trunk, then bent the knee of his good leg up toward his back and caught the ankle with his right hand. He tugged gently to stretch out his quadriceps.

"Usually five miles. I don't have time for more," she said.

A whoosh of air escaped his lips as he released his leg. "Then we'll run five today. Do you have some preferred routes you usually take?"

She nodded, pressing her left arm across the front of her body and holding it for the count of ten. "I measured the distance with my car's odometer the first week I arrived in town. Because of my move to Stokely, I wasn't able to run for a couple of weeks. I was eager to get back to it…and then I hurt my ankle."

"Yeah, I know what you mean. Exercise is addictive. I get antsy whenever I miss a day or two," he said.

So much for small chat. She kept warming up, concentrating on her movements, trying to think of something more intelligent to say. But maybe it was best if they stuck to the trivial stuff.

"I told Cade and Lyn about our plans to view Gilway Trail on Friday. They're excited about this project. So am I," he said.

"Good. Me, too." And she meant it. The thought of doing something positive to help the amputee kids at Sunrise Ranch gave her a good feeling inside. As if her life's work meant something important, even though she had no family to share it with.

She finished her warm-up routine and stood watching him.

"Shall we?" He indicated the black asphalt.

With a nod, she stepped off the curb and ran down the side of the street. He followed, keeping pace beside her.

At the corner, she looked both ways, then crossed the street and headed outside of town. Her body felt jittery, wanting to run faster than normal. She made a conscious effort to hold to her usual pace. Dal adjusted easily, his steady breathing a comforting sound beside her.

They didn't speak much until they reached the turnoff to Sunrise Ranch. Without breaking stride, Dal pointed toward the mountains on the south side. "That's the trailhead at Gilway."

"Okay, we'll take a closer look on Friday." As they reached the dirt road, she pointed at a yield sign. "This is my two-and-a-half-mile marker. Time for me to turn back."

He nodded and went with her.

"You don't have to return with me, Dal. You've probably already gotten in more than six miles today."

"I don't mind."

He kept running, and she had no choice but to keep up.

"You always were so persistent," she said.

He jerked his head toward her, his eyes narrowed slightly. "How would you know that?"

Her face heated up like road flares. Without thinking, she'd given herself away. She'd never been much good at pretending and she detested keeping secrets, with good reason. Something she'd been forced to do for eight months when she'd been barely sixteen years old. Until her social worker had figured things out and yanked Julie out of a horrible foster home. But not before her foster dad had hurt her and destroyed her faith in humanity.

Dal stopped dead in the middle of the road and lifted his hands to his hips. He looked at her, a mix of anger and relief covering his face. "Don't you think it's time we both stop pretending we don't remember each other?"

She released a gasp of air and came to a standstill. "I'm sorry, Dal. I—I didn't know what to say. I wanted to move on. I just didn't think it mattered anymore."

"Well, it does. And I've still got some questions you may not want to answer."

Her mind raced as she tried to slow her heavy breathing. Those old feelings of dread and fear seeped through every pore in her body. Like a caged and wounded tiger faced by a hunter carrying a loaded rifle. "Like what?"

"Like why you stopped writing me. And why you wouldn't return my phone calls. What happened, Julie? You just disappeared off the face of the earth. Why did you abandon me?"

Her gaze clashed, then locked with his. In his eyes, she saw all the anguish she'd caused him. All the pain she herself felt inside. "I never meant to hurt you, Dal. Please believe I didn't have a choice. Not really."

"No choice?" His voice escalated, betraying his anger. "You cut off all communication with me. Without any justification at all. Why?"

"I had my reasons. That's all I can say."

"You owe me an explanation, Julie. We didn't even break up."

"I thought it was for the best. We were living in separate towns by then and rarely saw each other."

"But we talked by phone almost every day. Until you stopped taking my calls. Why? Why did you do that?"

"I—I didn't want to talk about it then."

His mouth dropped open and he raked his fingers through his short hair, showing his frustration. "So let's talk about it now."

She shook her head. "No."

"No?" He sounded hurt and furious at the same time. "Oh, come on, Julie. You can't ignore me again. I'm here. Flesh and blood. You can't hide from me anymore."

She wanted to cry. To beg his forgiveness for hurting him. To crawl in a hole and hide. "Please, Dal. Let it go. Talking about it reminds me of ugly things I'd rather forget."

"So that's it?" His jaw hardened, a look of incredulity on his handsome face.

Julie wished she could give him more. Wished things could be so much different.

But they weren't. And they never would be again.

Tightening her resolve, she nodded. "That's it."

He hesitated, as though thinking this over. Standing in the middle of the road facing each other, the sound of rustling trees filled the void. After years of regret and longing for something more, Julie realized how utterly alone she was. She'd never felt so empty inside.

So hollow and bereft.

"No, I can't accept that," he said. "I have a few ugly things from my past I'd rather forget, too. But I want you to know something, Julie. After the last time I drove to Tulsa to see you for your sixteenth birthday, I never forgot about you. Not ever."

Oh, that hurt. Her stomach tightened with guilt and regret. He'd been so good to her, and look how she'd treated him. The only person in the world who had really cared about her. After what she'd gone through, she'd wanted to call him. So many times. To beg for his help. To ask him to take her away. But what could he have done for her? A kid from nowhere, just like her. They weren't even legal adults. With no money, no education, no real jobs and no way to change the life they'd been thrust into.

She wanted to tell him about it now, but couldn't. It wouldn't change the outcome. She couldn't confide in him something so horrible that just thinking about it caused her to shake as if it had happened only moments before. All the humiliation and embarrassment came rushing back. Right here, right now.

Instead, she turned and walked toward home. He fell into step beside her, silent and brooding. She felt his disapproval like a leaden weight. This discussion wasn't over. Someday soon, she knew she'd have to offer him an explanation. The silence soon became deafening.

"How's your mom doing, Dal?"

He lowered his head an inch, staring straight ahead. "Mom passed away while I was in Afghanistan."

His voice sounded harsh and indignant.

"I'm so sorry. She was such a dear woman."

"Yeah, she was. But I believe she's at peace now. Losing Dad when I was so young was always hard on her."

"Did you ever marry and have kids?" She shouldn't have asked, but she really wanted to know.

"No. I was engaged once, but…it didn't work out. She didn't want me after… After the war."

He glanced down at his leg, and Julie understood. His fiancée hadn't wanted him after he'd become an amputee. He'd become damaged goods, just like Julie. She wished Dal had found happiness with someone. He deserved a life of joy. So did she, but that didn't make it so.

She kept walking. Ignoring her wobbling knees. Wishing he'd leave her alone and forget they'd ever found each other again. It was easier that way. Less heartache. Less emotions.

Less to lose.

He stayed beside her. Just as relentless as the day she'd refused to go to the movies with him until he'd asked her out five times. Finally, she'd conceded out of frustration. And that had been the beginning of the best memories of her life.

But that was then and this was now. They couldn't go back. She couldn't get close to this man again. And that was that.

Why wouldn't Julie talk to him? Dal couldn't figure her out. All the past years stretched vacant before them, and she refused to offer a single explanation as to what had happened to her. Or why she'd turned her back on him.

Why she'd stopped loving him.

He remembered the night her parents had died with perfect clarity. The authorities figured her dad had been driving the car when they'd hit a deer on the dark interstate. Julie had been out on a date with Dal. They'd gone to the movies and then for cheeseburgers and fries at the local drive-in. Not wanting to face her dad's deep frown, Dal had brought her home five minutes before curfew...and found Sheriff Levy waiting on her front doorstep.

The weeks afterward had been a numbing whirl of grief. The funeral and burial. Julie had no other family. No one to provide her with a home. Dal had even begged his mother to take Julie in, but Mom couldn't. Working as a cook on the ranch where they lived, there was no extra room for Julie. Even with Dal's after-school job at the local grocery store, they barely made ends meet. Mom insisted that Julie would have a better life in foster care. Dal hadn't agreed, but he'd had little choice in the matter.

For a few months, Julie had stayed with a kind family in their hometown. She and Dal had been inseparable. She hadn't discussed her feelings over her parents' death, but he'd been there for her. Every day. Just to let her know he loved her and that everything would be all right.

Then the social worker had moved Julie to a foster home in Tulsa, eighty-seven miles away. It might as well have been eight hundred miles. At first, they'd written and called each other every chance they got. Not so easy without cell phones.

In thirteen months' time, the distance between them had done nothing to dim their love. Dal figured that was how it is when you find your soul mate. He even took the bus to visit her twice. He'd never forget her haunted expression or the way she'd clung to him when it had come time for him to leave. By then, she'd seemed so withdrawn and reserved.

That'd been the last time he'd seen her. Three weeks later, he couldn't reach her by phone. Her foster mom had told him she'd been moved and was living with someone else now, but she didn't know who. When Julie's letters had stopped coming, he'd called Social Services to see if she was okay. But they'd refused to tell him anything. It was confidential information, they'd said.

Dal had known something had happened to Julie besides her parents dying. Something bad.

In desperation, he'd convinced his mom to use her single day off work to drive him to

Tulsa. He'd gone to Julie's foster home, but the chilly welcome and lack of information drove him to Social Services. Their reception had been almost as cold. They wouldn't tell him where Julie was or who she lived with now. He wasn't a family member and had no right to the information. Driving all that way hadn't helped.

And so he'd gone home and waited. Relied on God to take care of her. Hating his youth and inexperience. Wishing he was a grown man with a life and a way to provide for the girl he loved.

Julie never called. Never sent him so much as a simple postcard to let him know she was alive. Not a single word in twenty long years. And now here she was. Without an explanation or apology. Without so much as a nod.

Why? Had she fallen for someone else? Maybe she was just angry at him for leaving her. For not being able to stay. But that didn't seem right. Before she'd been moved to Tulsa, he'd proposed they run away together. Julie had been the one to refuse. She wanted him to use his athletic abilities to get a scholarship and go to college. To make something of his life.

Instead, he'd gone to war and lost his leg.

Whatever had happened to Julie, he didn't understand. None of it.

"You must have gotten a college degree. I know it was always one of your goals," he said.

"Yes, but I didn't get the chance to attend a university until I was twenty-four. After high school, I got a summer job fighting forest fires in Oregon. I liked the work and being outside. So I decided to do something with my life and focused on my schooling. It wasn't easy, but I worked my way through with scholarships and student loans."

"I'm glad, Julie. You deserve some happiness in life." And he meant it. His love for her had been pushed to a small corner of his heart, but it had never dimmed. He wanted nothing but the best for her.

"Thanks. How about you? Did you ever get your football scholarship and go to medical school?"

He nodded. "For two years, but I didn't finish. You know I loved working with horses. I ended up joining the Marine Corps and seeing the world."

When he thought of all the death and blood he'd seen in battle, a scoffing laugh escaped his throat. He wasn't about to say that losing her had taken the joy out of his college plans. Without Julie, he'd had no desire to pursue the dreams they'd made together.

"I'm glad you're safe, Dal. I have nothing but admiration for all our military men and women."

He glanced at her, seeing the sincerity in her eyes. And that was when he knew he still loved her. In spite of everything, he couldn't be angry with her. Nor could he forget what she'd meant to him all those years ago. And knowing all that reminded him of why he could never be with her now. Life had changed them. Hardship had shaped them into the people they'd become. And his secret past would now keep them apart.

"Thanks for running with me, Dal." They'd

reached her front yard. The morning shadows had faded with the gleaming sunlight. The neighbor across the street came outside in his bathrobe to retrieve his newspaper.

"You're welcome."

Julie pushed open her gate, stepped past then closed it firmly behind her.

As Dal waited until she went inside her house, he longed to curse God. How could he accept this cruel twist of fate? Why, after all these years, had the Lord brought them back together? It seemed like a taunt. A spiteful prank played on him and Julie. It changed everything and nothing. And that was the cruelest part about this situation.

Chapter Four

The next morning, Dal showed up to run with Julie again. And the next. They settled into a comfortable routine. Warming up together. Chatting about the upcoming 5K race. The weather. Alterations for the horse trail and campsite. Workshops Dal had planned for the kids at the amputee camp. Everything but what was really on both of their minds. Why Julie had quit returning Dal's phone calls and letters once she went into foster care.

The following week, Julie drove her Forest Service truck out to Sunrise Ranch. Tall aspens lined each side of the graveled driveway, the spring breeze ruffling the leaves.

As she broke from the stand of trees, a panoramic view of the ranch opened before her. Nestled in the green valley, a variety of corrals and other ranch buildings surrounded the white two-story house. A spacious red barn, stable and gazebo sat on the south side. Compact cabins lined the outer perimeter on the north side, along with two large bunkhouses. Julie figured that must be where the staff and amputee kids lived when they stayed at the camp.

As she parked out front, she opened the truck door and looked to the east. Two men raced their horses across the green meadow. A blue-coated Australian cow dog zipped alongside the horses like a bullet. Though a goodly distance away, Julie had little trouble identifying Dal on a dun-colored horse. His confident carriage and the width of his strong shoulders were distinctive. He lay low across the neck of his horse, his right arm outstretched to give the animal full rein. The other man rode much the same way as their mounts sprinted toward the barbed-wire fence dividing two pastures.

A flutter of fear ruffled Julie's already frayed nerves. She clutched the handle of her leather briefcase with whitened knuckles. As Dal and the other man crossed an imaginary finish line, they pulled up short of the corrals. Julie released a shaky breath of relief. The dog plopped down in the grass, tongue lolling out of his mouth while he panted. By Julie's calculations, Dal had won the race by a full length. The horses slowed to a walk, and Dal clapped his friend on the back. Their laughter echoed off the tall mountains surrounding the ranch.

Julie sucked in a deep breath, trying to relax. For a moment, she'd feared Dal might crash into the fence. As he walked his horse toward the house, he looked her way, lifting an arm to shield his eyes against the glaring sun.

Julie's pulse sped into triple time. She could almost feel Dal's eyes boring into her like a high-speed drill. She couldn't help being highly aware of him as a handsome, masculine man. In high school, he'd been outgoing and athletic to the point of being reckless. But now he was older and should know better. Perhaps being an amputee made him think he had something to prove. And yet, she was impressed that he hadn't let his injury stop him from living a full, active life.

Knowing he could clearly see her truck, she feared that he might come over to visit her. She hurried toward the wraparound porch, eager to get inside the house. She'd be out here again tomorrow morning to ride with Dal up on the mountain to view Gilway Trail. That was soon enough to see him again.

She gave the front door several quick raps with her knuckles. A cute girl, about twelve years old with an adorable button nose, answered her call.

"Good afternoon. Is your mother home?" Julie asked.

"Yeah, come on in." The girl stood back to let Julie step inside.

Julie's gaze lowered to the girl's legs. Dressed in a pair of knee-length shorts, the child also wore a prosthetic leg. Like Dal, she walked without a hint of a limp.

"Mom! The new ranger's here," the girl yelled over her shoulder.

"Oh, my goodness. Is it that time already?" a woman's voice called from the kitchen.

The house smelled of cinnamon and warmth. Something nice must be baking in the oven.

"You must be Kristen," Julie said to the girl. She knew Lyn and Cade Baldwin also had a new baby.

"Yes, and you're Dal's old girlfriend," Kristen said. A statement, not a question.

Julie's jaw dropped. Her mind churned, wondering what Dal might have told these people about their past. "We were good friends once."

"I love Dal, too. He's one of my best friends in the whole world."

Too? The girl must think Julie still loved him. And Julie didn't know how to disabuse the child of that notion without offending her.

"Dal saved my dad's life," Kristen said. "They were in the war together. Of course, Cade's not my real dad, but I love him like he is anyway. Cade was a prisoner of war, and Dal went in to get him free. Dal pushed him out of the way during an explosion. That's how Dal lost his leg. The bomb hurt him real bad. I lost my leg in a car crash that killed my real dad."

"Ah, I see. It's a good thing Dal was there to save Cade." Julie blinked at this detailed information. Kids were so guileless, open and honest. Julie knew Dal had lost his leg in the war, but hadn't known he'd done it while saving another man's life. No wonder he and Cade Baldwin were such good friends. Hearing about Dal's heroics made Julie feel emotional and patriotic. She had no doubt God had sent Dal to rescue Cade. But now she wondered if Dal needed rescuing.

"Have a seat. Mom will be right here." Kristen walked back into the kitchen.

Resting her briefcase on the floor, Julie sat on the edge of the closest chair to wait.

A soft baby blanket had been tossed over the armrest, and she pushed it to one side as she looked around.

Braided rag rugs covered the shiny hardwood floors. A large stone fireplace dominated one wall of the tidy living room. Woven baskets with colorful, intricate designs decorated the tabletops, along with vases of dried field flowers. A striking Native American headdress made of ermine and rabbit fur rested atop a tall armoire. Beautiful pictures of wild mustangs and modern cowboys adorned the walls. A playpen and a basket of toys sat in the middle of the room.

Obviously the Baldwins favored a Western motif. Julie had been told by her office manager that Cade Baldwin was part Shoshone Indian and ran a medical practice three days a week in town. Julie could find no fault with this comfortable home and had great respect for the work Dr. Baldwin and his wife did for amputee kids.

A scuffling sound came from the kitchen, and then an attractive woman with long blond hair and warm brown eyes appeared in the doorway. With a flustered sigh, she used a damp cloth to scrub an orange splotch of what looked to be baby squash off her shirtfront. Tossing the dishcloth onto the kitchen table, she came forward with a bright smile. "I'm so sorry. I lost track of time. I just finished feeding the baby."

"Is this a bad time to talk?" Julie asked as she stood.

"No, of course not. It's always crazy around here. I'm Lyn Baldwin, and you must be Julie Granger." She extended her arm.

Julie returned the woman's smile as they shook hands. "Yes, I'm glad to finally meet you. I've got so many questions I'd like to ask."

"Sure. I'll help any way I can. Please sit down and relax." Lyn indicated the chair.

"Thank you." Julie sat. "Do…do you need to get your baby?"

"No, Kristen's with her."

At that moment, Kristen came into the

room carrying a chubby infant wearing a pink sundress and a full head of dark, curly hair.

Julie fell in love immediately.

Lyn pointed at the girl. "You've already met my daughter, Kristen. She's twelve. And the little one is Clarisse, my other daughter. She's seven months old now and getting her first teeth."

Kristen jostled the baby on her hip. "Do you want to hold her?"

No! Julie knew nothing about holding a baby, but the invitation caught her off guard. "I, um, sure."

Kristen handed the infant over, and Julie clutched the little girl around the middle with both hands. Little Clarisse hung suspended in the air, sucking on her fist. She gazed at Julie with wide blue eyes. And then the baby laughed. An exuberant chortle that made Julie blink in surprise.

"Hey! She likes you," Kristen said.

"She sure does." Lyn curled her bare feet beneath her and sat on the leather sofa.

Julie didn't know what to say. Didn't know

what to do. Prickles of panic rushed up her throat. She hadn't held a baby since…since she couldn't remember when. But as she looked into the eyes of this innocent little being, so vulnerable and trusting, Julie's insides dissolved into mush.

"Do you have kids?" Lyn asked.

"No, I've never married."

"Well, you're a natural mom. Anyone can see that."

A creeping heat stole its way over Julie's face. She'd given up on marriage and kids long ago, but that didn't mean she didn't want them. Life just hadn't provided them. Not with her aversion to most men. So she'd learned to settle for what she did have.

As Clarisse kicked her bare legs, Julie couldn't help cuddling the little girl close within the crook of her arm. A domestic feeling of tenderness flooded Julie's heart with regret. How she wished she could have…

No! She couldn't think that way. It wasn't fair to torture herself over something she didn't have. Instead, she focused on the good in her life. Like right now, sitting in this comfy home with a baby in her arms.

Clarisse waved her tiny hands and made several happy panting sounds, shredding the rest of Julie's resistance. She snuggled Clarisse close, catching the clean scent of her skin. Before she could think to stop herself, Julie brushed her lips against the baby's soft forehead in a spontaneous kiss.

Dallin Savatch chose that precise moment to walk through the front door. Another tall, dark-haired man accompanied him.

Julie flinched and sat up straight, feeling startled and exposed.

"Howdy." The stranger flashed a smile.

"Hello." Julie tensed, trying not to let Dal's intense gaze snag hers as she focused on the other man.

"Julie, this is my husband, Cade. And I believe you already know Dal," Lyn said.

"Y-yes. I'm pleased to meet you, Dr. Baldwin." Old feelings of discomfort washed over Julie. She felt suddenly inappropriate, as if she'd done something wrong. She didn't belong here with this wonderful family. She didn't belong anywhere. She should have asked Lyn to come into town to meet at her office. There, Julie wouldn't have to cuddle a cute baby. There, she could keep her wits about her and a measure of control.

And avoid Dal's penetrating eyes.

"Hi, Julie." His deep voice filled the air, as though he resented her being here.

She should leave. Right now.

His gaze dipped down to the baby and then back up to Julie's face. His shoulders tensed, and in his eyes, Julie saw something. A flash of reservation. She wasn't sure. As if he couldn't believe she was sitting here holding an infant.

Julie couldn't believe it, either.

"Clarisse really likes you," Cade said.

"Yes, it's incredible, isn't it?" Lyn agreed.

A shiver of nervousness bristled down Julie's spine. "Why is it so amazing?"

"Clarisse won't go to just anyone," Dal said. "She usually screams her head off. Even I can't get her to let me hold her."

"Oh. I'm sorry."

"Don't be. I'm glad she likes you." He

coughed and looked away, as though he'd confided too much.

Standing, Julie handed the baby back to Kristen. "I think she needs her diaper changed."

Okay, it was an excuse. A pretext to let go of the baby and focus on her work. After all, that was why she'd come here today. Not to make friends, and certainly not to bond with someone else's children.

A buzzer sounded in the kitchen, and Lyn hopped off the couch. "You men are just in time. The first batch of cookies is done. I'll be right back."

Lyn disappeared into the kitchen.

"I'll go change Clarisse." Kristen carried the baby down a hallway toward the back of the house.

Alone with the two men, Julie felt a stutter of confusion. This meeting wasn't going quite as she'd planned. She and Lyn were supposed to be alone, to quietly discuss Forest Service issues.

"Dal tells me you're old friends from high

school." Cade slumped back on the couch, his smiling gaze on her face.

She glanced at Dal, feeling uncomfortable. "Yes, we knew each other once."

"How do you like your new job?" Cade asked.

Dal continued to stand beside the door, his hands in his pockets, his ears slightly red.

"Very well, thank you. There's a lot to learn, but I'm enjoying it so much," Julie said, glad to be talking about anything but her and Dal's past relationship.

Cade chuckled and crossed one leg over his opposite knee, looking casual and relaxed. "Don't worry. You'll pick it up soon enough. Most of the ranchers in the area are pretty reasonable. Lyn can give you some pointers on how to cope with those who are more difficult."

Good. That was the kind of information Julie needed. Not babies and cookies and hazel-eyed men from her past.

"Here they are. Fresh and hot from the oven." Lyn entered the room carrying a tray with a plate of cookies and glasses of milk. The tantalizing aroma wafted through the air.

During the next fifteen minutes, they all sat and consumed the soft oatmeal-raisin cookies. For the most part, Julie and Dal remained silent while Lyn and Cade kept up the conversation. They discussed the new horse trail and campsite, the expected timeline and what work might be required. Kristen returned and handed Clarisse over to her daddy. Cade smooched the infant's neck, then endeavored to feed her small pieces of cookie. Clarisse gummed the crumbs with a great deal of enthusiasm and her parents laughed. Even Julie couldn't resist cracking a smile.

"Dal tells us you dated in high school," Lyn said.

Julie wrenched her gaze around, wondering if there was anyone on this ranch who wasn't going to ask her the same question. "Um, yes. That's right. But that was a long time ago."

"It must be fun to meet up with an old boyfriend after all these years," Lyn said.

Julie didn't respond, struggling to keep the smile pasted on her face. She rested one hand along the armrest of her chair, fingering the downy softness of Clarisse's baby blanket.

"I think it's time I got back to work. I'll see you tomorrow morning." Dal stood and, with a quick nod toward Julie, headed for the front door.

Cade released a sigh of resignation. "Me, too. Nice to have met you, Julie. I'll look forward to working with you on our trail project."

He kissed Clarisse on the forehead, then handed the baby over to her mother.

"Yes, the horse trail should be quite an adventure." Julie tried to sound positive when she was feeling the complete opposite.

In turn, Cade kissed his wife on the lips and Kristen on the forehead, then left, pulling the door closed behind him.

Julie breathed a silent sigh of relief. With the men gone, her racing nerves settled back to a normal pace. No matter how nice they were, being around men made her nervous. They just did.

Especially Dal. Although for different reasons she didn't dare contemplate.

Eyeing Julie's briefcase, Lyn made a suggestion. "Why don't we go into the kitchen so we can use the table? Then we'll have room to spread out and talk."

"That's a great idea."

"Kristen, will you watch Clarisse for a little while?" Lyn asked.

The girl nodded and slipped her arms around the baby.

As the women stood and made their way into the other room, Julie reminded herself that this was her first ranger district, and she was eager to perform to the best of her ability. She was educated and experienced and knew how to do her job. Outside of work, she didn't want to get involved with Dal and his best friend's family. Next time—if there was a next time—she'd ask Lyn to come into town to meet with her there.

Remembering her jogging commitment with Dal, Julie inwardly groaned. As it stood, she would be forced to spend more time with Dal every morning. Unless she did something to change that.

Maybe it was time she purchased a treadmill to use inside the comfort of her own home. She could make some kind of excuse to Dal, but knew that might hurt his feelings. Plus, she didn't want to do that. She hated admitting it, but she liked running with Dal. And that was just the problem. For twenty years, she'd purposefully avoided any personal attachments. A lone woman apart. But that had changed in a matter of weeks. Because, like it or not, she now cared what Dal thought. And caring about a man scared her most of all.

"You're awful quiet," Cade said.

Standing inside the stable, Dal barely spared the other man a glance as he picked up a pitchfork. Max, Cade's Australian cow dog, lay nearby, panting.

Dal pitched hay to the horses. "I don't have anything to say."

"You didn't tell me she was so pretty," Cade said.

Dal looked up and tried to keep his expression blank. "Who?"

Cade tossed a handful of straw at him in a teasing gesture. "Julie, that's who. And don't try to pretend you don't know who I'm talking about."

With a shrug, Dal set the pitchfork aside and reached for a bucket of oats. "Yeah, I suppose she's pretty enough."

"You suppose?" Cade stared in surprise. Then his mouth quirked in a knowing smirk. "Oh, I see. You loved her. Just how serious was your relationship with her when you were in high school together?"

Dal flinched. He couldn't help himself. But he didn't say a word.

"You don't want to tell me about it?" Cade asked.

"Nope." Dal walked the length of the stable, his boot heels pounding against the floorboards in rhythm with the beat of his heart. Hoping Cade would give up on the topic and leave, Dal stepped inside the stall of one of their mares.

Cade followed, and so did Max. When they all stopped, the dog slumped down on the floorboards while Cade cupped his hands over the top handle of a manure rake. "You told me she's single. Are you gonna ask her out?"

"Nope." Dal set the pail down with a muffled thump and patted the mare's neck as she lowered her head to eat.

"Why not?"

A feeling of helpless anguish crushed Dal's chest. "You know I don't date. Not for years now."

Cade snorted. "I'm not asking you to marry the woman. Just go out and have some fun for a change. What could it hurt?"

Dal shot his best friend a withering glare. "I can't afford to take the chance, Cade. What if she falls in love with me? You know I have nothing to offer a woman. I'd only break her heart."

"Are you afraid she'll fall in love with you, or that you might fall in love with her?"

"Both," Dal growled. "The outcome would be the same. Broken hearts."

He stalked over to the grain barrel and scooped oats into another bucket.

"That's hogwash," Cade said. "Julie isn't Barbara. I can tell after one meeting that Julie's not the kind to dump you just because you have a prosthetic leg."

Dal lifted his brows. "Barb dumped me for more reasons than just my leg."

Cade released a disgusted huff. "She always was a superficial witch. I never liked her."

"That's harsh. You hardly knew her."

"I knew enough. But Julie is different. I saw the way she looks at you. She doesn't even notice your leg. She's too busy trying to avoid your eyes. She blushed at least a dozen times while you two were together. She likes you. A lot. And you like her. So why not ask her out?"

Dal slammed the bucket down on a plank workbench, and Cade flinched. "It's not that simple, Cade, and you know it. If it were just a matter of dealing with my prosthetic leg, I could cope with that. But the IED caused more damage than that. I may never be able to father a child. You think I want to saddle Julie, or any woman, with a husband like that? Julie deserves kids. Lots of them. And I may not be able to give her that. I can't give her anything."

A heavy silence followed Dal's outburst. Dal hated discussing his dark secret. As a result, very few people knew the truth. And Dal preferred it that way.

The two men stared at each other. The best of friends. Closer than two brothers could ever be. And yet, Dal stood alone in his misery.

"You'll never know, unless you try. Isn't the possibility of a happy life together worth giving it a shot?" Cade asked.

"No. I can't take that chance. I won't put Julie through that," Dal insisted.

A horrible, swelling silence followed.

"Look, Dal. You saved my life when we were in Afghanistan." Cade spoke in a slow, soothing voice. "I've never forgotten how you came in with the special-ops team to rescue me when I was a prisoner of war. You pushed me out of the way and took the brunt of that explosion yourself. Otherwise, I wouldn't be here today. I owe you everything. And I can't stand to see the toll that sacrifice has taken on you. You have the right to be happy, too. You can have a fulfilling life with one special woman. You don't need kids for that."

Dal shook his head, his mouth tightening with his ghastly memories of war. "I've never once regretted saving your life, Cade. I never will. But did you just see Julie holding Clarisse? That woman deserves kids of her own. I don't have a choice, but Julie does. She deserves so much more than I can ever give her."

"Why don't you let Julie decide that for herself?" Cade said. "Usually a woman marries a man because she loves him, not for the children they might have together."

"Yeah, and can you picture me asking her out? I can hear me now. Excuse me, Julie," Dal's voice took on a mocking tone, "but I may not be able to father a child. Would you go out with me anyway? We don't need to fall in love or marry. Let's just have a good time. And if we ever get serious, you'll just have to live with disappointment. How does that sound?"

An abrasive laugh slipped from Cade's throat and he clapped his hands, as if in applause for Dal's performance. "Bravo. Very nice. But cynicism doesn't become you, buddy. You know, there's always adoption."

"And what if Julie doesn't want to adopt? What if she wants to have kids of her own? If I married, how long before my wife starts to resent and hate me?"

"If she really loved you, it would never become an issue," Cade said.

Dal lifted his brows. "Oh, really? Can you predict the future, then? I thought Barb loved me, but she took one look at my amputated leg and ran for the hills, screaming. I think she would have tolerated the prosthesis, but when she heard the rest of the news, that was it. She didn't love me enough. And I can't blame her."

Turning, he jerked on a pair of leather

gloves, then reached for a bale of straw and half dragged, half carried it to one of the clean stalls. Cade did likewise. Dal wished the other man would just leave him alone.

"You're right," Cade said. "Barb didn't love you. Not really. Not if she couldn't see the great man you are in spite of losing your leg."

Dal snorted. "I'm tired of this worn-out topic."

"Remember when you first came to town?" Cade asked. "I was avoiding going out with Lyn, and you gave me some good advice. Do you remember what you said?"

The grating sound of Dal grinding his teeth together was his reply. But yes, he remembered as if it was yesterday.

"You said, you care for that woman and she cares for you. Nothing else matters." Cade paused for the count of two. "You also told me to take her flowers. Daisies, because they wouldn't come on too strong until I asked her out. Do you remember? Julie's different from Barb. You said she lost her parents and ended up in foster care. She might be the one woman to understand and see you for the great man you really are."

Filled with a surge of anger, Dal lifted the bale up and heaved it into the stall. The binding around the bale broke and straw spewed everywhere. As Dal drew back, he nearly stepped on Max, and the dog skittered out of his way. "Yeah, half a man. That's what she'll see. That's all I'll ever be."

Cade set his bale down and dusted off his hands. "You're more than that, but you just won't see it."

"We're supposed to go up and view Gilway Trail in the morning. I'd rather you went with Julie instead of me," Dal said.

"No dice. I've got clinic duty. Lots of patients coming in. You'll have to go with her." Cade smiled.

Dal whirled around and stared at his friend. "You can wipe that smirk off your face."

"And you should ask Julie out on a date."

"And you should mind your own business," Dal groused.

"Maybe we could double-date. Lyn would love that. And it would make conversation easier until you and Julie catch up on everything…."

Dal slashed the air with his hand, cutting Cade off. "Leave it alone. I mean it. Let it go."

Turning, Dal stomped out of the stable and headed toward the meadow. He hoped Cade wasn't following him. The way he was feeling right now, Dal might sock his best friend in the face. And then he'd have to explain to Lyn why he'd blackened her husband's eye or broken his nose.

To make sure he was alone, Dal tossed an angry glare over his shoulder. Cade stood with Max beside the watering trough, both man and dog watching Dal with a look of grave concern. Thankfully, Cade had the common sense to stay put this time.

Dal kicked at a clump of grass. It wasn't that he didn't appreciate Cade's efforts. In fact, just the opposite. But, in the end, it didn't make any difference. Dal would love nothing more than to date Julie, fall deeply in love and marry her. But life hadn't been kind to either of them. They both carried a cruel past they were each trying to stash in the attic and forget.

Dal loved Julie. He always had. And because he loved her, he never wanted to hurt her again. Which meant no dates. Not ever. Not for him.

And that was that.

Chapter Five

Dal didn't show up to go running with her the next morning. Julie knew she hadn't accidentally missed him because she peeked past the curtains in her living room just before dawn. For almost two weeks now, he'd stood leaning against the tall cottonwood on the other side of her fence just as the sun came up, waiting for her to join him. She'd dubbed it "his tree." But he wasn't there today. She delayed her jog an additional ten minutes, but still he didn't show. She'd come to enjoy the quiet camaraderie they'd shared. And though she'd never admit it out loud, she couldn't help feeling a bit disappointed and confused.

Two hours later, she stood in the Forest Service corral loading Dottie, her appaloosa mare, into the horse trailer. Maybe Dal hadn't gone running with her today because she'd be seeing him later that morning. They'd spend most of the day together, surveying Gilway Trail. She feared that his absence went deeper than that. Yesterday, when they'd eaten cookies at Sunrise Ranch, she'd sensed his reticence. His reluctance to be near her. In the beginning, he had been the pursuer and she had been the one who wanted him to stay away. Now it seemed to be just the opposite. She wanted to be near him all the time.

A mere twenty minutes later, she pulled into the driveway at Sunrise Ranch. Without announcing her presence, she lowered the back tailgate and unloaded Dottie. She'd just tossed a blanket over the mare's back when Dal came out of the stable riding a buckskin gelding. The man wore a scruffy cowboy hat, tight blue jeans and scuffed boots. Handsome and tall in the saddle. Even from this distance, she felt his intense gaze, and her senses kicked into overdrive.

"Morning." He greeted her with a curt tug on the brim of his hat.

"Good morning," she replied. "I missed you for our run today."

Now why did she say that? She should have let it go. He didn't owe her any explanation. So why did his absence this morning bother her so much?

He pulled up and leaned one forearm against the saddle horn. "Sorry, I should have called you. It's been rather hectic this week. We've got our first group of kids this season coming in next Monday and a lot to do yet."

She didn't understand why that had kept him from running with her at five-thirty this morning. She tried to read between the lines, but found no answers. Something had changed between them, and she sensed that it had to do with her visit to the ranch yesterday afternoon. "So soon? I thought you had a couple more weeks before the start of camp."

He stepped off his horse, showing no indication that he was hampered by his prosthesis. "Nope, it's next week, and we're still a bit short on kitchen staff. I've been trying to find someone to help serve meals in the evenings, but not many people in town are willing to work after five o'clock. Most have families of their own they need to tend to."

"What about high school students looking for summer employment?"

"If they were hardworking and patient with our kids, we'd hire them on the spot. But only one student applied, and we hired her. We need a couple more."

"Have you advertised in the local newspaper?"

"Yeah, and I also put up fliers in the grocery store, gas station and post office. No bites yet. But we'll make do."

She envisioned cute amputee kids like Kristen swarming the ranch next week and thought it might be fun to see.

His gaze flicked past her spruce-green pants and the bronze shield pinned to the left front pocket of her Forest Service shirt. "I can't get used to you in that uniform."

She brushed her hand down one sleeve of her crisply ironed shirt and smiled. "I know. This drab olive isn't my best color."

"No, it's not that. I keep remembering you in your cheerleading uniform."

"White and royal blue, with big, puffy pom-poms," she said.

"Yeah, you were so fun and easygoing in those days. Now you seem so…so official."

Was she so different now? She supposed life had changed them both in too many ways to count. "I'm here in an official capacity, but I'm still a nice person, Dal."

His gaze locked with hers, but still he didn't smile. "I have no doubt about that."

At that moment, Cade and Kristen walked out onto the front porch of the house and waved.

"Good morning!" Cade called.

"Morning," Julie returned with a smile.

"Hi, Julie." Holding a brown paper lunch sack in one hand, Kristen looped her backpack over her shoulder and gripped the handrail. A subtle indicator that she was in a hurry and didn't want to stumble on the stairs with her prosthetic leg.

Funny how Julie now noticed such things in the short time she'd spent with Dal.

"Sorry we can't talk now. We're running late." Cade's keys jingled in his hand as they rushed down the steps and headed toward his truck parked nearby.

"I understand. Have a nice day," Julie called.

"We will, and you two have fun," Cade said.

Dal thrust a thumb in Cade's direction. "He's late for the clinic and has to drop Kristen off for her last day of school before summer break."

"Ah." Julie wondered how this busy family kept up with all they had going on. "You sure you have time to view Gilway Trail today? We can postpone."

Julie paused as she reached inside the horse trailer for her saddle, waiting for Dal's response. No sense in saddling her horse if they rescheduled their trip.

Letting the reins on his gelding trail on the ground, Dal brushed past Julie and lifted the saddle before placing it onto her horse. "I'll make the time today. This project is important for next year's camp."

With swift movements, he cinched up her saddle, then dangled the reins over her forearm.

"Thank you." She gripped the reins with white knuckles, wondering about his abrupt manners. On the one hand, he was being polite and gentlemanly. Considerate of her needs. On the other hand, his brusque gestures told her he was irritated about something. She figured she was the cause, though she wasn't sure why.

At least not yet.

"You're welcome." He didn't smile as he returned to his horse.

Julie stared at his wide back. The tension in his shoulders and his clipped words spoke volumes. Something was bothering him. Something big.

In the back of her mind, she couldn't help wishing he'd flash that dazzling smile at her one more time. It was on the tip of her tongue to remind him that he'd approached her about developing Gilway Trail, not the other way around. But then she decided to remain professional. Shut up, do her job and go home. She didn't want to be friends with this man again. She didn't care about his troubles.

Or did she?

They stepped up into their saddles and headed out, loping their horses across a meadow of new grass and blue lupines. Julie took a deep inhale. Being outdoors always brought her a measure of peace. She loved nature and the thrill of working in the mountains. For a time, she could almost forget the sadness that still haunted her after twenty years. She could almost believe that God still loved her.

Almost.

Within twenty minutes, they reached the trailhead. Julie pulled her horse up and rested her left hand against the cantle of her saddle. Dal sat silently nearby, letting her look at the layout as he awaited her judgment.

"Right off the bat, I can see that the opening to this trail isn't in compliance with accessibility requirements," she said.

"What do you mean?" He pushed his hat back on his head. His horse swished its tail at a fly and stomped a hoof.

"I doubt that trail opening is at least thirty-two inches wide, that is, wide enough to accommodate a wheelchair." She indicated the two gray boulders that stood like sentinels, framing the entrance to the thin path beyond. "It wouldn't take much to move these rocks and widen the opening with some heavy machinery."

He quirked a brow. "The trail is awful steep to make it fit for a wheelchair."

"We won't be modifying the trail for a wheelchair, just the opening." Reaching for a small notebook and pen she kept in her shirt pocket, she jotted a few notes.

Dal leaned forward, his brows pulled together. She felt uncomfortable with him watching her so closely.

"How do you plan to get your kids mounted on their horses?" she asked.

He narrowed his eyes in thought. "Back at the ranch, we just use step stools. One of the staff members is always right there to help out each child. Almost one-on-one attention, to ensure the kids' safety."

"A step stool will be a bit impractical way out here," she said. "We could easily install a livestock ramp, so your kids czan lead their horses up to the side and then climb on more easily. A small bulldozer could fit in here to build a dirt ramp right there. Along the trail, you'll still need a stool, in case one of the kids needs to get off their horse for some reason."

"A ramp would definitely cut down on the number of stools we need to bring with us. I like your idea," Dal said.

"Handrails are probably impractical in this environment, but we can install some on the ramp. Once the kids get on their horses, they should be okay." She stepped off her mare and tied the reins to a nearby tree branch.

Dal did likewise, his head tilted as he listened to catch her every word. Julie felt jittery with him following so close, but decided to focus on her work. She was in her element and knew what she was doing. A handsome man from her past shouldn't make any difference.

But he did. She couldn't deny it.

"Right here, I suggest we install several hitching rails for your horses. You'll need one over by the ramp, too." She gestured as she spoke. When she turned around suddenly, she ran smack into his wide chest.

"Whoa! Excuse me." He lifted his hands to clasp her shoulders.

Julie stumbled, but his strong grip kept her from falling. His face flushed scarlet as he settled her, then backed away.

"Sorry, Julie."

"No, thank you. It seems you're always saving me." She gave a nervous laugh, trying to lighten the moment. Trying to ignore the buzzing in her head and the sizzling energy that pricked her skin where he'd touched her arms.

He glanced at her boots, then stared blankly at the ground. The coward.

She took a deep inhale and caught his scent of spice and leather. How could a man smell so nice?

She slammed the door on that thought. He was just a man after all. A very kind, attractive man.

"Um, there's plenty of room for you to bring in a truck with supplies, if you decide to do that. But you'll have to use pack horses from here on." She continued with her dialogue, trying to pretend she hadn't almost run him over. "You can't use any motorized vehicles along the trail."

She made more notes, noticing that Dal now kept his distance, his warm gaze following her every movement.

"We'll put a sign kiosk right here, out of the way." She pointed at a shady spot beneath the spread of cottonwoods. "It'll include the name and length of the trail, the grade and slope of the path, and some rules associated with use of the campsite. A map might be a good idea, too." She pointed at a rock wall at the base of the mountain. "We'll want to avoid changing this natural cliff formation. It's attractive, and we don't want to alter anything we don't have to."

"If you say so." He nodded and slipped his hands into his pants pockets, a look of hesitation in his eyes.

Shy and reserved. Not at all like the outgoing, playful boy she'd known in high school.

Reaching into her saddlebag, she pulled out a camera and started snapping pictures.

"What are those for?" Dal asked.

She tilted the lens to get the right angle on a particular incline. "So I can remember the exact setup of the terrain once I get back to my office. The pictures will also help once we hold our public meeting. I want to be prepared for anything."

"I dread that meeting," Dal said. "Some of the ranchers in the area are dead set against any development of this trail. They seem to think our kids might invade their privacy somehow."

She snorted. "I don't see how that's possible. You're the only rancher in this vicinity. The next ranch is two mountains over."

"Still, they may fight the development."

She nodded. "And I'll listen to their objections. But that doesn't mean we won't proceed with the work. This is a good cause. I'll be impartial and reserve my final call until I've seen the entire layout. But so far, I see no reason not to alter this trail."

Not if she could help it. As a teenager, she'd needed someone to make a difference for her. That someone had been Berta Alvey, an elderly widow who had taken her in after she'd lost all trust in men. For two years, Berta had worked with her, helping her see that not everyone was willing to take advantage of a young orphan. Now Julie believed the work she was doing for the amputee camp was important. She wouldn't go against any Forest Service regulations, but she was also determined to help Sunrise Ranch in any way she could. For the benefit of the kids.

As she snapped several more pictures, she tried to tell herself her goal had nothing to do with Dal. That she didn't care about pleasing him, too. But she knew that wasn't true.

Dal took a deep inhale and looked up at the cottonwoods swaying in the breeze. "Wow, it's pretty up here."

"Yes, it is," she agreed.

"Whenever I view the beauty of the earth, it deepens my belief in God."

She didn't respond, and he glanced at her.

"Don't you feel the same?" he asked.

"I definitely love the outdoors. That's why I chose my profession." That and so she could be by herself. Sexual abuse had a way of making a person antisocial.

"I don't see how anyone can look at God's creations and not believe in Him," Dal said.

She shrugged. "Maybe God has let them down."

Dal spun around and gazed at her with surprise. "Surely you don't mean that."

She made a pretense of jotting more notes. "Berta believed in God."

He lifted one brow. "Berta?"

"My last foster mom before I graduated

from high school. She took me to church every Sunday. She insisted that I stay out of trouble and go to college. Even after I was an adult, she would still hunt me down to make sure I was living right." She chuckled at the memories.

"She sounds like a great lady."

Julie nodded. "She was."

"Was?"

"She died a year after I graduated from college, but I was so glad she got to see that day. I owe her everything. If there is a God, then He sent Berta to me." Her throat suddenly felt dry as sandpaper.

"Then you don't believe in God?" An edge of disbelief tinged his voice.

She shrugged. "God and I kind of just leave each other alone these days."

"You used to love God. Before your folks died, you went to church with them every week."

And sat in the back pew with Dal's arm looped around her shoulders. She'd been so content in those days. So calm and happy. Then tragedy had struck.

"Yeah, well, that was before Mom and Daddy died." And that was all she was going to say about that.

"I know you've had some hard knocks in your life," Dal said. "So have I. But God's been there with me every step of the way. Without Him, I don't think I would have survived the war. After I returned to the States, I wanted to die. God sent a special friend to me, just as He sent Berta to you."

Listening to Dal speak, Julie could almost believe what he said was true. That God had been with her through her darkest days. "Cade was your special friend?"

"Yes, but he needed help, too. As a prisoner of war, he survived some pretty cruel torture. But after I lost my leg, he wouldn't let me quit, even when I begged him to let me die."

She gave a sad little smile, realizing how much they both had in common. "Yes, that sounds like Berta. She never gave up on me, even when I screamed at her and made her life so difficult."

Julie wanted to believe the Lord cared for

her. That she wasn't alone in this big old world. But if that were true, why had God taken her parents from her? Surely God didn't need them more than she did. But then, God had sent her Berta. And Janice Baker, her old boss with the Forest Service. Janice had put Julie on a wildfire crew as a summer job. Later, the woman had mentored Julie as she'd made her way through college and built her career in the Forest Service. Janice and Berta had made a great difference in Julie's life.

Maybe it was now Julie's turn to give something back. To make a difference for a child in need.

"You said you're shorthanded in the kitchen for your evening meal shift," she said.

He nodded, looking quizzical. "That's right."

"I'd like to volunteer to help out a couple of nights each week, if that's all right."

Oh, now she'd done it. She waited for a sick feeling to settle inside her stomach, a warning that she'd pushed herself beyond her comfort zone and would live to regret it. But that feeling didn't come. Not this time. She didn't want to retract her offer. In fact, she felt almost driven to help out at the amputee camp. Almost as though her future happiness depended on it.

Dal stared at Julie for several moments, considering her offer. After his conversation with Cade yesterday afternoon, he'd been ready to call and cancel this excursion up Gilway Trail with Julie. To forget the whole plan. But something had kept him from doing that. Something he couldn't explain. As if he just physically could not pick up the phone, dial her number and say the words.

Working on the horse trail was one thing, but letting Julie help out in the kitchen back at the ranch was another matter entirely. She'd be constantly underfoot, spending a lot more time working with him. He hadn't gone jogging with her that morning for a good reason. He needed to put some distance between himself and this woman. If she started working at the ranch, he'd be with her even more. And right now, Dal didn't know if he could take that. In fact, he was certain he couldn't.

"Not everyone likes working with amputee kids. They have special needs. It's a lot of hard work," he said.

"I understand, and I think I'd like it."

Great. Now what?

He blew out a breath. "How about if we try it for one week. If it's not working out after that time, no hard feelings. Agreed?"

There. He'd given both of them an out. A week would give him some extra time to find a replacement. Then he could thank Julie graciously and call it a day. She'd return to the Forest Service office in town, and he'd remain secluded back at the ranch. No more jogging together. No more quiet talks and gazing at her lovely profile. No more warmth and fuzziness between them.

No more danger to his heart.

"Agreed." She flashed him a smile so bright it made his throat ache.

She whirled around and stepped toward

the trailhead. “Now, back to work. This trail will be a Class Two, single-tread trail.”

She jotted more notes, and he wondered how she could act as though nothing had just happened. The thought of seeing her next Monday night flooded his entire being with nervous energy.

“What does that mean?” he asked.

“It’s a minimally developed trail for pack and saddle. Used primarily for hiking and horses. That means we’ll need a greater clearing width for switchbacks and turns, so your horses can pass and turn more easily.”

Good. That was just what he had in mind.

She looked up the mountain and clicked another picture. “I can see from this slope that jogging and bicycling would be practically impossible, but some people ride their mountain bikes anywhere.”

Dal didn’t care about mountain bikes, as long as they didn’t interfere with his kids on their horses.

“Let’s ride up the mountain. I want to see the area you’d like to develop for the campsite." Julie headed for their horses, a new lightness in her step.

Had agreeing to let her help out at the camp made her this happy? If so, he couldn't bring himself to put a damper on her generosity.

They stepped up on their horses, and Julie led the way toward the trail. The path was rather steep, and the horses grunted as they climbed higher. When they reached a wider area along the trail, Julie pulled up and peered out over the tops of ponderosa pine and Douglas fir. The mountainside looked like a carpet of green, sloping down to the valley below.

"It is so beautiful here," she said.

He was gazing at her. "It sure is."

She glanced at him, and he looked away before she could see the hunger in his eyes. The longing to tell her how he really felt about her. In all these long, lonely years, he'd never stopped believing that they had unfinished business between them. But now it was too late.

She pointed uphill. "We're gonna want to

avoid steep grades where possible. Nothing over eight percent, except on the switchbacks."

"Okay." He barely heard her words. His ears felt clogged, as if he was submerged under water.

When she nudged her horse forward, he followed. As they rode, he tried to focus on her observations. Tried to shove his deep feelings into a remote corner of his heart and abandon them there.

She pointed at a barren switchback, rocky soil void of any vegetation. "This will be an erosion problem. A few rock and log barriers along the edges will prevent people from shortcutting across the path and keep the trail in good condition."

He coughed to clear his voice. "You think we can get a bulldozer up this far to widen the trail?"

She shook her head. "No, we'll use hand tools to widen the path. Adding more switchbacks will do a lot to make the trail more comfortable."

Hand tools would require a lot of back-breaking labor, but he trusted her judgment.

Higher up, the trail widened out and Julie pulled up again. "This might be an excellent place to install a bench and hitching rail. There's plenty of room for your kids to stop to rest and enjoy the view. We might even be able to build a step for them to use for remounting."

Now why hadn't he thought of that? Her insight impressed him. "That'd be great. We sometimes have kids who tire quickly. Knowing there's a bench midway up the trail will give me a way to entice them to hang on a bit longer."

When they reached the open area for the campsite, they both dismounted. Dal's horse danced away, and he stumbled. His left hand wrenched free of the saddle horn, and he fell backward on the uneven ground. As he hit the dirt, his breath was knocked from him in a giant whoosh. He gasped to fill his lungs with air.

"Dal! Are you okay?" Julie rushed to his side.

He sat up in stunned embarrassment. Julie was watching. He felt so clumsy. So foolish. "I— I'm fine. Really."

"Let me help you." She gripped his arm, but he shook her off.

His pride crumbled, and he locked his jaw. "I can do it by myself."

His harsh words startled her and she stepped back, her mouth dropping open in surprise.

"I'm okay, Julie." He tried to soften his rebuff, but hated the guarded look on her face.

He rolled over onto his good knee and reached for the stirrup to pull himself up, but the horse jigged away. Down on all fours, Dal's face flushed with heat. Embarrassment covered him from head to toe. He refused to look at Julie, wishing with every fiber of his being that she wasn't standing there witnessing him like this.

He tried to get traction on the uneven ground, but his good foot kept slipping in the loose soil. He'd be forced to crawl over to a tree in order to stand.

With Julie watching.

Out of his peripheral vision, he saw her reaching for the reins before she pulled his horse near. The stirrup dangled in front of his face and he latched on to it, pulling himself up. As he got back on his feet, he reached down to adjust his prosthesis. Luckily the socket hadn't come loose from his stump. The last thing he wanted was to ask Julie for privacy so he could pull his pants down and readjust the C-Leg. Right now, he felt exposed and vulnerable enough.

Unmanned.

"I just want to help, Dal," she said.

He didn't look at her. "I know. I didn't mean to snap at you."

"It's okay. Sometimes it's hard to accept someone else's help, even when we need it. I also have a lot of trouble admitting I'm not invincible and in control every minute of every day. When I fall down, I hope you'll help me up, too."

He didn't smile.

"Do you always have trouble accepting help from others?" she asked.

"No, just you."

She tilted her head to one side. "Why is that?"

Back on his feet, he gave her a slow grin. "You really need to ask?"

"Point taken. But I hope you'll get rid of such silly inhibitions. We used to be best friends, once."

Yes, he was hyperaware of that fact, but decided to ignore the situation. Confessing that he needed this beautiful woman's help tweaked his pride. Because he loved her. Because he wanted to show her that he was a man. Strong and virile and in control. And he wasn't. Not really.

To change the topic, he pointed at the clearing surrounded by a stand of aspen. "We'd like to install six cabins up here with a large fire pit in the center for gatherings and roasting marshmallows. Is that possible?"

She blinked, as though it took her a few moments to mentally change the subject. Morning sunlight glinted off her long chestnut hair.

"We can build a fire pit, but no cabins. That's too permanent. We can construct tent pads, though. Each pad will be approximately ten feet by twelve feet. This campsite will follow a pack in, pack out policy. Anything you bring in, you must also take out. Nothing left behind." She locked her gaze with his as she spoke.

Dal realized she meant what she said. The professional forest ranger was back, ready to follow regulations. "Yes, ma'am. Can we at least have a couple of outhouses?"

Again, she shook her head. "I'm afraid not. Pit toilets only."

"Pit toilets?"

"Yep. We don't want to alter the nature of the outdoor experience any more than necessary. Each pit toilet will have a riser between seventeen and nineteen inches off the ground and a toilet seat, but that's it. You can construct tent walls around each toilet, to offer privacy. But the walls have to be removed each time you leave the campsite."

He gave a shrill whistle. "Wow. I hadn't

planned on that. You really want us to rough it, huh?"

"Call it camp setup. When you first arrive, get your kids to help with the work. Give them assignments and attach groups of them to a leader. Setting up should be part of the camping process. You want an outdoor experience for them, and I don't want to damage this natural setting. Win-win for both sides."

He chuckled. "Win-win? I'm not so sure I agree with that."

Her expression softened. "It'll be great for the self-esteem of your kids. Not a lot of coddling will make them earn their experience out here in the mountains. And when they get home, they'll talk about it for years to come. Use the buddy system. Have the kids help each other. They'll build relationships to last a lifetime."

Her understanding of what he and Cade wanted to accomplish for the kids surpassed even Dal's expectations. Here he was, wishing he could have a comfy cabin and outhouse to use, and she was giving him ideas on how to get the kids to work together. To grow and learn. To become stronger individuals, in spite of their amputations. When Dal considered her suggestions, he couldn't help feeling impressed by her acumen.

"You've become an amazing woman, Julie Granger." The words poured out of his mouth before he could call them back.

"Back at you. You're the most remarkable man I've ever met."

A knot of apprehension settled in Dal's throat, and he coughed several times to clear it. It wouldn't budge.

As they rode back toward the ranch, he realized that one of the last things he wanted in this world was to be considered remarkable by Julie Granger.

Chapter Six

Julie stood looking at the panoramic view below. Mountains blanketed by limber pine and aspens spread out before them, their leaves shivering in the warm breeze. Lake McClellan lay nestled in the valley below. Sunlight shimmered off the pristine waters like a trillion diamonds. Julie felt as though she could almost reach out and scoop up a handful.

A lovely scene that normally brought her peace. But not today. Not right now. Her guilt haunted her with memories. Reading Dal's letters. Listening to his pleading voice mails before deleting them with no response. She owed him an explanation, yet couldn't offer one. It was too embarrassing. Too humiliating to even think about.

The crack of a stick behind her reminded her that she wasn't alone. Her breath stuttered to a halt. He stood behind her. Waiting. The only man she'd ever loved.

He touched her sleeve. "Are you okay?"

His deep voice thrummed through her, making her long to turn and curl into his arms. To offer her cares over to his capable hands. To let him be her confident captain.

"Yes, I'm fine. I was just admiring the beautiful view." She wrapped her arms around herself, feeling cold in spite of the warm, sunny day.

"Then why don't you join me for a bit of lunch?"

She didn't move. Just stood there, the breeze blowing a wisp of hair across her face.

He bumped his shoulder against hers. "Come on, sit down and talk with me. You can tell me anything you want. I'll keep your deepest, darkest secrets forever. I'm a steel trap." He deepened his voice to a teasing purr, but she caught his serious undertone.

She tilted her head and watched as he sat on a fallen tree trunk. He patted the seat beside him and waggled his eyebrows. "It's waiting just for you. I offer nothing but the best out here in the wilds. No table and chairs, but at least the view is stupendous."

A laugh slipped from her throat. She longed to confide in him. To trust him. From what she'd observed, they both needed a confidant. Someone to unburden their hearts on. But they wouldn't. At least not today.

She joined him on the log where he presented her with a single blue lupine. As she took the stem of the delicate flower, her fingers brushed against his. Warm tingles washed up her arm.

"Thank you." She breathed the words.

"You're welcome." He met her eyes.

Julie stared at him for several moments, mesmerized. Longing to reach out and cup his cheek with her hand. Instead, she looked at his chin, where she could see the slight shadow of his beard. He hadn't had much facial hair when they'd been teenagers. The sharp slant of his cheekbones and accompanying stubble fascinated her.

She looked away, forcing herself not to stare. Side by side, they ate their sack lunches. An easy silence settled over them. It always amazed Julie that she felt so comfortable being with this man. With Dal, there was no need for pretense or to make conversation. Because of their past, she now felt nervous and unsure of herself.

No boats dotted the surface of the lake today. Julie knew that would change once school let out for the summer. Her Forest Service work crews had seeded the lake last Thursday with seven-and eight-inch trout. The kids at Sunrise Ranch and other anglers would have a blast catching them.

A movement down by the lake caught Julie's attention, and she reached for the binoculars she kept in her daypack. Looking through the lenses, she focused on a deer standing beside the shore near the narrow boat dock. Julie pointed it out for Dal.

The gentle animal dipped its head down for a cool drink of water. Then, as if sensing the two people watching it from above, the deer bolted, its spindly legs leaping over fallen tree trunks and low-lying boulders.

"Do you use the lake for the amputee camp?" Attempting to start a conversation, Julie handed the binoculars to Dal, then took a bite of her turkey sandwich.

Dal lifted the binoculars to his eyes and swallowed a bit of potato chip. "Yes."

"Kayaking and swimming?"

"And fishing."

She quirked her brows. "No water skiing?"

He lowered the binoculars. "No, it's too expensive to buy and maintain speed boats. Besides, the kids who have both their legs are usually missing a hand or an arm. And the kids who have their hands are usually missing a leg. We've discussed using an inner tube to pull the kids on, but we don't have any extra funds to buy a boat right now."

"Oh." She hadn't thought about these issues. Any time she reached to pick up something or walked across the room, she took her hands and legs for granted. She couldn't help admiring Dal's determination to live with his amputation. Of course, he didn't have a choice. But he did. She'd heard reports of broken soldiers returning from the war and committing suicide. The thought of Dal taking his own life tore her up inside. She couldn't stand to even think about it.

The brooding silence continued. Julie glanced at Dal, taking in his tensed shoulders. The clipped words when he spoke. Nothing had changed between them since they'd started their trip that morning. Everything about him told her to go away. They both kept forgetting to be on guard. Like when Dal had given her the flower. But then they'd remembered the past, and both of them put up their barriers again.

She couldn't blame Dal for being standoffish with her. She knew she'd hurt him years ago. But now she felt drawn to him more than ever. As though he needed her. Which was odd, considering he'd even refused her help for something as simple as getting up after falling off his horse. But she sensed that he was deeply troubled. Because of her. She didn't know why. Her first instinct was to take the hint and leave him alone. Her dislike of men was justified. But that didn't seem to matter now. Not with Dal anyway. She felt certain that he needed her in spite of his reticence. And that didn't make sense at all. The Baldwins were his family now. Julie could see no future for the two of them. At least not as a couple. But maybe, after all these long, lonely years apart, it was finally time she made one lasting friendship.

"What time Monday do you want me to show up for work at Sunrise Ranch?" She bit her lip and watched to see his expression.

His face darkened, and she thought he might back out. "As soon as you get off work. You'll hit the ground running. I guarantee we'll keep you busy."

"I'll be there as soon as I can get off work."

"Okay."

She heard the resignation in his voice, and her heart squeezed hard. All she could think about at that moment was how sorry she was for ever hurting this man when they were sixteen years old.

Now he was all alone, just like her. No doubt his amputation had isolated him to a certain extent. And that sent a shiver of sadness skittering down Julie's spine.

"You deserve to be happy, Dal."

"Everyone deserves to be happy, Julie. You included."

She gave a slow shrug. "I am happy."

"Even being alone?"

Her heart shot up to her throat. A buzzer went off inside her head, warning her that this was a taboo subject that would yank them both out of their safety zones. "Most of the time. What about you?"

His head dipped down. "Most of the time."

He didn't say what they both must be thinking. Yes, they were happy, but there were times when an aching loneliness settled over them like a damp blanket.

Whether they admitted it or not, they both needed someone, anyone, to love them for who and what they were. Dal was a talented, desirable man. In spite of his amputation. In spite of his limitations.

Okay, those thoughts were no good. She was out of her depth here, in danger of drowning. Her thoughts touched the lonely place she kept buried deep inside. Opening her hidden feelings to the light of day would only bring her more pain. But something told her she must not walk away from him again. Not this time.

She smiled and nudged his arm. A playful gesture she immediately regretted. But she'd always felt so relaxed around this man. Even before she'd loved him like crazy. "Dal."

He looked at her, his eyes wary. "What?"

"Don't worry about my helping out at the ranch. I'm not going to hurt you again. I promise." And she meant it. She mustered every ounce of willpower to show the truth on her face. Trying to win his trust again.

He blinked, then took a brief, settling breath. "I sure hope not."

Dal brushed a shaking hand against his prosthesis. After his fall, he'd felt stupid and inadequate. Like a joke. Now, listening to Julie's vow not to hurt him again, he didn't know how he felt. His lips parted to speak, but no words came out. His tongue felt as though it had been stapled to the roof of his mouth.

He tried again. "I think it's time for us to go home now."

"Yes, I'm eager to write up my report while everything is still fresh in my mind." She hopped up, gathered the wrappers from their lunch and placed them in a paper sack to pack off the mountain.

He stood, the trembling in his limbs finally abating. He felt strong and in control again. And yet, it was a facade that deepened the emptiness in his heart. All it took was one faulty step and he'd be lying face-down in the dirt, struggling to get up again. Crawling across the ground like a lowly animal.

"Where did you finally graduate from high school?" he asked as they got on their horses.

"Robert's High School, in Tulsa."

"I always wondered who took you to your senior prom. Remember that green dress you wanted to buy?"

She flashed a sad smile. "Yeah, but I didn't go."

A sharp pang of regret stabbed his heart. "Me, neither. I didn't want to take anyone but you. But I can hardly believe no guys asked you out."

"A couple of them asked, but I…I didn't feel like going."

He wanted to ask why, to tell her she could have gone with him, if she'd just kept in touch with him. But somehow, he knew even that wouldn't have mattered.

He settled himself in the saddle, clutching the cantle with one hand. "You should have gone and had fun dancing."

She looked down, gathering the reins in her hands. After a moment, she looked up and met his gaze, a faraway look in her eyes. "I…I had a bad experience with one of my foster dads, Dal. He…he hurt me real bad. That's why my social worker pulled me out of that house."

A heavy weight settled on Dal's chest, and he swallowed. He didn't want to know, but was compelled to ask. "What happened?"

She turned her head away, and he thought he saw the sparkle of tears on her cheeks.

"I…I can't believe I just told you that. But I'd rather not talk about it, Dal. It's an ugly memory I'd rather forget."

Dal sat there motionless. Unable to move. Unable to breathe. He wasn't stupid, and his imagination ran wild. And then he felt regret like a claw ripping his heart to shreds. If only he'd been there, he might have been able to protect Julie. To keep her safe. He tried to imagine how she felt. How she'd coped with her life. It had been so unfair to both of them.

"I don't have the answers to everything, Julie. But I do know there's no hurt in the world the atonement of Jesus Christ can't heal."

She looked at him, her warm brown eyes seeing deep into his soul. "I want to believe that, Dal. I really do. And I'm trying. But I hope you'll take your own advice."

His breath rushed out of his lungs, as though she'd just slugged him in the gut. She'd always been so blunt. Calling his bluffs. Hitting the nail on the head. He shouldn't be surprised that she'd turned the tables on him. He'd been trying to help her and, in turn, she'd given it right back to him.

If only she knew the truth, she might think differently. He'd gotten on with his life. He'd healed. But he couldn't change the inevitable. Accepting his own limitations was easy, but he wouldn't foist them off on her. He couldn't bring himself to tell her his own deep, dark secret.

As they rode back the way they'd come, the afternoon sun waned into early evening. Spending time with Julie up on Gilway Trail had been eye-opening, to say the least. Even so, it didn't change anything between them.

At least not for him.

Chapter Seven

She was late. Work at the office had kept her after hours. Dashing out of the Forest Service building on Monday evening, Julie raced home to change her clothes. She didn't want to wear her ranger's uniform to help serve food at Sunrise Ranch. Next time, she'd remember to take her street clothes to work with her and change there.

On the drive out to the ranch, she tried to keep within the speed limit. Her pulse skipped into double time, a bead of perspiration dotting her forehead. She tried to tell herself her nerves had nothing to do with seeing Dal again. That she was just keyed up over the work she'd volunteered to do at the camp. She knew it was so much more than that.

She parked her car in front of Lyn and Cade's house and threw the door wide-open. Sprinting past the gazebo where the kids worked on their art projects, she raced to the dining hall. The buzz of voices and the rattle of dishes met her ears as she darted into the kitchen. A beehive of activity engulfed her. She came up short at the threshold, breathing in the pungent kitchen aromas of garlic, tomato sauce and dishwashing soap.

Adults wearing bright red T-shirts that read Staff across the backs stood at a counter with a glass panel, serving food as kids filed by with their trays. More adults were positioned beside two enormous stainless-steel sinks, scraping plates and washing enormous pots and pans and utensils. Swarms of amputee kids sat at the long tables in the hall, eating their dinner. Their happy laughter mingled with the loud chatter. Excited voices filled the air as the kids made new friends and discussed the upcoming activities for the week. Julie couldn't blame them. Free from their parents for a whole week, they were understandably excited and pleased with this new adventure. Normal kids in every way, except that each one had an amputation of some kind.

Wearing a variety of leg, arm and hand prosthetics, some kids used crutches, walkers and canes as they made their way through the food line. One little girl with legs but no arms received help from a camp instructor. Her lack of limbs didn't seem to hinder the child in the least. She hopped up and down with excitement, laughing as one of the other kids tugged playfully on her two long braids.

Julie's heart gave a poignant squeeze, and she tried not to stare. She couldn't explain it, but she wanted to hug each and every child and tell them how much she loved them. Except for Kristen, she didn't know any of these kids, yet she cared what happened to them. A Christlike love that filled her with compassion. She couldn't explain it better than that.

"Julie!"

She turned and saw Dal standing in front of the industrial-size stove, stirring the contents of a tall, silver pot. Dressed in his usual blue jeans and cowboy boots, he also wore a long white chef's apron over his black T-shirt. She couldn't resist smiling at this masculine man in such garb.

Relieved to see someone she recognized, Julie slipped past the other workers and sidled over to him. "Hi there. Sorry I'm so late."

His gaze skimmed over her ponytail and plain work clothes with approval. "It's no problem. Thanks for coming. We can sure use your help tonight."

His words warmed her heart. It felt good to be needed. "I'm glad to help. What do you want me to do?"

Lifting his hand, he gestured toward a closet. The wooden spoon he held dripped a creamy white soup mixture into the tall pot. "We've got some extra aprons inside there, and you can stow your purse out of sight."

She did as he asked and retrieved an apron similar to the one he wore. When she walked past him, he snapped his dish towel at her hip. She gave a nervous laugh, trying to ignore his teasing smile as she looped the top of the apron over her head. Dal came up behind her to secure the ties at the small of her back. She held perfectly still, the firm movements of his hands tugging on the apron making her jittery.

"How are you at cooking?" he asked, his warm breath brushing against the nape of her neck.

She shivered, in spite of the summer heat.

"Not very good," she answered honestly over her shoulder. "Berta taught me to boil water and use a microwave, but that's about it. I can't cook at all."

Returning to the stove, he quirked one brow. "Can you stir a pot to keep the contents from burning?"

"Of course." She flashed a half smile.

"Good, you can stir the soup while I get another batch of rolls in the oven." He reached in front of her to grab a set of oven mitts for his hands, and she caught his warm, clean scent.

His nearness reminded her of the cooking class they'd taken together in high school. She hadn't learned a thing, but she'd had so much fun with him. Laughing. Feeding each other spoonfuls of tapioca pudding. Making plans for the rest of their life together. That had been an idyllic time. A naive time, before real problems intervened.

She picked up the long-handled wooden spoon he'd abandoned and stirred the pot. Her gaze followed his graceful movements as he lifted a heavy baking pan filled with rounded gobs of dough, opened the oven door and slid the pan inside. Almost simultaneously, he pulled a hot pan of golden-brown rolls out of the oven and slapped it onto a wooden countertop to cool. A warm, yeasty aroma filled the air. With a quick twist of his wrist, he set the timer. After a couple of minutes, he flipped the cooked rolls into a large basket lined with a clean cloth.

"You've become so domestic," she said.

"If you think this is domestic, you ought to see what I can do with apple pie and lasagna." He waggled his eyebrows at her as he carried the basket of rolls to the front counter for the kids to consume.

Julie laughed, amazed to see him moving around the kitchen like a seasoned pro. More and more, she realized that his prosthetic leg was no hindrance at all. When she realized she was staring at his biceps, she jerked her gaze away and listened as he called to the kids.

"Come and get them. Hot out of the oven."

Several children hobbled over, and he teased them as he set some of the warm rolls onto their plates.

"You guys hungry?" he asked as he worked.

They all nodded, their faces wide with grins.

"Well, eat up and have fun. Get lots of rest tonight, because I'm gonna keep you very busy tomorrow."

The kids just beamed.

This was the Dal Julie knew and remembered. Happy. Outgoing. So filled with life. When she thought about the boy she'd loved, she could see him now in the handsome, competent man he'd become. Losing his leg hadn't dimmed his masculine appeal. Not for her.

She looked away, her smile fading. The urge to trust Dal waged a war with her fears. She'd confided in him, but getting closer than that wasn't in her plans. It wasn't that she thought he'd ever hurt her. But after what her foster father had done, she just didn't think an intimate relationship was for her. Not with any man. And that left her feeling sad and lonely. Emotions she'd grown comfortable with.

Until recently. Lately, she found them a nuisance and even wished she could put them aside for good. To move on with her life.

With Dal.

No! She shouldn't be thinking such thoughts. Not at her age. Romance had passed her by long ago. She was a career woman now.

Dal returned to her side just as a loud crash caused her to jerk her head around.

Through the glass counter, she saw two boys in front of the tables. One boy around ten years old with bright red hair lay sprawled across the linoleum floor. His prosthetic leg was twisted at an odd angle that told her it had come loose from his stump when he'd fallen. His tray of food lay splattered across the floor. A second boy, a couple years younger with coal-black hair and missing his left hand at the wrist, stood over him, laughing.

"Ha, ha! You're so clumsy."

"You did that on purpose!" the fallen boy yelled as he pushed himself into a sitting position. He brushed at his shirtfront, which was covered with mashed potatoes and gravy.

"Did not," the other child called in a belligerent tone.

Stationed in the dining hall, Lyn handed Clarisse off to Kristen, then raced over to the fallen boy. "Eddie, are you all right?"

She knelt down to help Eddie adjust the socket around his stump. Thank goodness the boy was wearing knee-length shorts, which made the prosthesis more accessible.

Two staff members Julie didn't recognize scurried over to pick up the broken dishes and clean up the mess. The other kids stared, watching the argument with wide eyes.

"He's clumsy, that's all," the belligerent boy crowed loudly. "He needs to watch where he's going."

"You tripped me," Eddie insisted through angry tears.

With an exasperated huff, Dal slapped his oven mitts on the counter, then jutted his chin toward Julie's pot of soup. "Keep stirring, Jules. I'll be back."

Her jaw dropped as she watched him head for the door. She stirred furiously as he rounded the counter and sauntered into the cafeteria to deal with the two boys.

Jules. He'd called her Jules. She hadn't heard that name since…since the last time he'd come to visit her in Tulsa for her sixteenth birthday. No one else had ever called her Jules. Just Dal. Hearing him use the name now made her feel all warm and fuzzy inside. As if she'd come home after being gone for years and years. Since Dal was her only living tie to her past, she supposed she had come home, in a way.

To him.

She shook her head, slamming the door on that thought.

"Marcus, did you trip Eddie on purpose?" Dal stood in front of the dark-haired boy and placed his hands on his hips, a completely male stance.

"Nah, he just tripped. He's a clumsy ox," Marcus said, his impish smirk a dead giveaway to his mischief.

By this time, Lyn had Eddie back on his feet, her arm wrapped around his shoulders. The boy sniffed, his eyes red, tears streaming down his freckled cheeks.

"You stuck your foot out and tripped me. You did it on purpose," Eddie cried.

"Did not," Marcus yelled back.

"Yes, you did. I saw you," a little girl interrupted.

"Marcus, come with me, please," Dal said.

The man stood back, giving the boy room

to precede him out the door. Marcus's features tightened, his eyes narrowed with anger. For a moment, Julie feared he might refuse to go. He was too young to take Dal on, but his eyes hardened with fury. She had no idea how parents dealt with their naughty children. This situation was completely alien to her.

Thankfully, Marcus obeyed. He stomped outside with Dal, glowering at everyone as he passed. The other children looked away, not meeting his eyes. Julie couldn't help wondering why the boy acted so hatefully. Had losing his left hand done this to him, or some other form of neglect or abuse by his parents?

She pondered her thickened soup, wondering what she should do with it now. Should she turn off the heat and try to carry the heavy pan over to the counter, or wait for Dal to return?

Lyn came to her rescue.

"Hi, Julie. I'm so glad you're here. We'd be lost without you tonight."

Julie doubted that, but gave a pleased smile.

"Put these on and help me carry the pot over to the counter so we can ladle it out for the kids." Lyn handed Julie the oven mitts Dal had discarded earlier, then found a second pair for herself.

Together, the two women gripped the wide handles of the heavy pot and lifted it off the stove. They slowly moved it across the kitchen to the serving line.

"Look out, coming through with a hot pot." Lyn called the warning to the kitchen staff.

Several men and women scrambled out of the way as Lyn and Julie set the large soup pot down at the front counter.

The buzzer rang, and Julie raced over to pull the rolls out of the oven, copying Dal's movements exactly. Once she had the rolls taken care of, she found herself standing at the counter, ladling creamy broccoli soup into bowls. The kids grinned up at her, and she couldn't help smiling back. Though she didn't speak, she found their enthusiasm infectious. They were so young and vulnerable. A warm, full feeling settled in her chest.

She felt happy to be here. Happy to be doing a good deed for these kids.

Though she wore no visible scars on her body, she knew how easy it was to break a child's fragile innocence. The thought made her feel incredibly protective of each one of them. Even though they were all strangers, she'd do almost anything to shield them from being hurt. And she couldn't help but wonder what was troubling Marcus to make him so unkind. Out of all these kids, she thought perhaps he needed the most help.

"I thought you said you couldn't cook."

She flinched and found Dal leaning over her shoulder. She stared at the dark stubble on his chin, his sudden nearness bringing a wave of dizziness to her head. She clutched the rim of the pot to steady herself.

"I can't cook. You made the soup. I just stirred it."

His lips twitched with a suppressed smile. "It's just a mix, so I can't really take credit for making it. Not from scratch anyway."

He took up a position beside her, scooping out green salad with a pair of tongs.

"Is everything okay with Marcus?" she asked in a muted tone, not wanting the other kids to hear.

"Yeah, Cade's with him now, mucking out one of the horse stalls."

Was that what parents did, then? Give their kids chores to do when they misbehaved? She tried to imagine how a one-handed boy could muck out a stall with a shovel. Her confusion must have shown on her face.

"Don't worry, Jules. Cade's good with kids. He'll help Marcus. They'll work together, and Cade will talk to the boy about what he did. He'll also talk to Marcus about the horses and things Marcus is interested in."

"That's a unique form of reprimand."

Dal nodded. "It works. When one of the kids does something wrong, we don't just give them extra chores to do as punishment. We actually stay with them, working beside them to give one-on-one attention. I'm afraid Marcus needs it more than most kids do."

Ah! She now understood the concept. If anyone deserved some one-on-one time, it was surely an amputee child who might be thinking his whole world had ended now that he'd lost his hand.

"I'm amazed you're able to deal with these kids. I'd be overwhelmed by them all," she confessed.

"And I don't know how you deal with angry ranchers and grazing permittees. That would scare me much more," he quipped. "In fact, I'm worried about the open meeting you have planned to discuss Gilway Trail."

"Because of the ranchers?"

"Yes. Some of them are dead set against it. They don't like us because our kids are different."

"You mean because of their prosthetics?"

"Yep. Being different frightens some people."

She snorted. "Surely they've got more reason than that."

He lifted one shoulder. "Nope, that's about it. They're good old boys who've been around forever and think they own everyone else. These ranchers can be pretty difficult at times."

"Don't worry, Dal. I'll handle them."

"I hope so." He looked doubtful.

"Is Eddie okay?"

"Yeah, nothing hurt but his pride."

Having watched Dal fall a few days earlier, she imagined he understood Eddie's embarrassment all too well.

"We've had nothing but trouble from Marcus since he arrived at camp this morning," Dal said. "He keeps starting fights with the other kids and acts argumentative every time we ask him to do something."

"I'm sorry. Is there anything I can do to help?"

Dal shook his head. "Nope, but I'm afraid it's gonna be a long summer."

"Why?"

Dal's gaze scanned the room of happy, chattering kids. "All the other children will stay at the camp for just five days, then they'll return home to their families. We have weekends to ourselves, to rest a little and get ready for the next batch of kids who come in on Monday mornings. But Marcus is a special case. His social worker asked us to keep him all summer long, and we agreed. He won't be going home until school starts up again in the fall."

"Why not?"

He jerked a shoulder. "Marcus doesn't have a home to go to."

"What do you mean? Surely his parents will miss him," she said.

"His parents were killed in a plane crash five months ago. Marcus is an orphan living in foster care. He hasn't adjusted very well, losing his parents as well as losing his hand."

Julie's heart sank to the floor. She wasn't an amputee, but she certainly understood how it felt to lose both her parents at once and end up in foster care. "Oh, the poor kid."

"Yeah, and the social worker thought being here at the camp all summer long might help build his self-esteem. Because of what we do here and who we are, we agreed."

She tensed. "Do you regret it? Would you rather send Marcus away?"

Dal pressed his lips together in a stubborn expression. "Absolutely not. If any of these kids needs us, Marcus does. I'm not about to turn my back on him, no matter how much trouble he causes. I just hope we can get through to him before summer ends."

Julie took a painful breath and held it in for several moments. Dal's reassurance brought her a modicum of peace, but her heart ached for Marcus's plight. She knew how it felt for people to turn their backs on her. To give up. To quit.

To abuse her.

"Thank you, Dal. I'm so glad you're the kind of man to stick with that little boy. I know it might be difficult, but you're right. Marcus needs you. He needs all of us. And what is life for, if not to serve others?"

Reaching for another large bowl of salad, Dal slid it into place and flashed her a wide grin. "Be careful, Miss Granger. You're starting to sound like the Savior."

Julie looked away, not knowing what to think about that. But she was willing to silently concede that maybe, just maybe, Dal was right.

Two hours later, Dal left the fire pit where Cade was directing story time. The kids sat with the staff members, roasting marshmallows to squish between squares of chocolate and two graham crackers. Marcus had knocked some of the kids' marshmallows off their sticks into the fire and been a general pain. Yelling, causing fights, upsetting the other children. Lyn had finally taken him to sit with her and Clarisse on the lawn chairs under the gazebo a short distance away. The boy had settled right down, showing a unique gentleness with the baby as he listened to Cade's stories.

Now Dal skirted past the stables, checking the horses one last time for the night. Then he made a detour over to the dining hall, planning to lock it up tight.

A light gleamed from the open kitchen doorway. He stepped inside.

Smack. Swish.

Julie stood in front of the wide refrigerators, mopping the linoleum floors. She twirled the heavy mop around an area, then dipped it into the sudsy water, sloshing it up and down to rinse it out. With her back to him, she smacked the stringy mop into the wringer and pressed hard on the lever. Water gushed through the holes on the wringer plate. She released the lever and slapped the mop back onto the floor before swirling it around another section.

He watched her closely. Studied her. Guessing at what she'd alluded to when she'd told him about her past. Wishing she would confide everything in him, yet knowing that would only bring them closer together. And neither of them could afford that right now.

As she struggled over a particularly dirty spot, her brows pinched together. He gazed at her sweet profile, adoring her. While all the other staff members were out at the fire pit gobbling down s'mores, she was still inside working. She'd always been like that. So dutiful. So wonderful. And he loved her for it. Loved her fierce spirit and determination.

He should turn around and leave. Right now. This very minute. Loving this woman would do neither of them any good. But he stood right there, leaning against the doorway, his hands in his pants pockets. Walking away from her felt wrong somehow, but he couldn't help that. To stay would take too great a toll on both of their hearts. And yet, leaving her hadn't gotten any easier now than it had been twenty years ago.

"You gonna work all night?" His whispered words filled the quiet room like a shout.

Julie winced, losing her grip on the mop. It clattered to the floor, and she spun around to face him.

"Dal. Hi there. You startled me." She sounded flustered and out of breath.

"Sorry. I didn't mean to." He moved away from the doorway and stepped inside.

"I thought you'd be out at the fire pit with all the kids," she said.

"I was there for a little while. Then I got hungry."

She quirked one brow. "Hungry?"

"For ice cream. You want some?" He walked over to the freezers, making sure he didn't step on the damp floor where she'd just mopped.

"Um, I really should be going. It's getting kind of late." She picked up the mop and stuck it back into the bucket for one final rinse.

"There's always time for ice cream," he said. "Leave the bucket. I'll dump the dirty water outside in a while. It's too heavy for you to lift anyway." He held his breath, hoping she wouldn't skip out on him now, yet half hoping she'd leave.

She abandoned the mop there and waited by the front counter until he brought a bucket of Neapolitan flavors over for her inspection.

The lid made a sucking sound as he pulled

it off. "We've got chocolate, strawberry, vanilla or all three. So which will it be?"

She reached for two clean bowls. "All three for me. Remember when you used to take me to the drive-in for banana splits?"

His chest tightened. "Yeah, I drove Mom's beat-up old Cadillac, and we ate all the ice cream we could get."

"I could afford the calories back then." She laughed, the sound bright and cathartic to his ears.

"You still can. You're running enough miles every morning to burn off anything you might eat."

"True. Fill 'er up."

He reached for a scoop and pulled it through the silky ice cream, giving her two large scoops. She held the bowl, not eating.

"You still jogging every day?" he asked.

"Yes. And you?"

"Yep. Sorry I can't run with you in the mornings anymore."

"That's okay. But I plan to whoop you on the day of the 5K race, so be warned." She gave him a mischievous smile.

"You're on, lady."

He didn't look up as he scooped ice cream into his own bowl. He took a bite of chocolate, enjoying the thought of running with her on race day.

"I got the advertisement for the open meeting on Gilway Trail all prepared and submitted to the local newspaper office. It should be out the day after tomorrow," she said.

"When's the meeting going to be?" He knew this meeting was a necessary part of the trail alterations, but it still worried him.

She told him the date and time. "But don't worry. I've studied your plans and see no reason we can't proceed with the work. I'll be prepared to answer some difficult questions."

They sat on stools and dipped their spoons into the icy treat.

"I'm worried about the cost," Dal said. "Cade and I can do a lot of the work ourselves, but we don't have lots of funds."

She licked a smudge of ice cream off the

tip of her index finger. "I've got a solution for you already worked out."

"Oh? What is it?"

"The Back Country Horsemen. I've already made some phone calls, and they're willing to help with both manpower and money. They've been wanting to do some work on this trail for a long time. And when I told them about your horse camp for amputee kids, they were in right then. It's for a good cause after all."

"The Back Country Horsemen?" He'd heard about them, but didn't know much about their group.

"Yes, they're a nonprofit organization that loves riding their horses along the backcountry trails throughout America. One of their goals is to assist with maintaining our wilderness trails. The local chapter is out of Elko, and they think developing Gilway is a good thing. Of course, once the work is finished, they'll want to use the trail, too. We'll coordinate with them so your kids aren't staying in the campsite when the BCH wants to use it."

"That's terrific. I didn't expect this, Jules. Thank you for going the extra mile for us."

"You're welcome." She flashed him a smile that lit up her eyes and made his throat ache with longing.

He couldn't do this. Shouldn't do this. Being alone with her, eating ice cream, talking to her about nothing and everything… It all made him think of what he couldn't have. A home. A family. A future. With her.

He stood up too fast and stumbled.

"Dal!" She reached out to steady him.

He regained his balance and stepped back, his arm prickling from her touch. "I'm okay. It's really getting late. I'd better finish my chores."

His words gave her the cue. She slid off the stool, then rinsed their bowls and placed them in the dishwasher.

"Thanks for the ice cream." Her voice sounded small and unsure.

She hugged herself, as though she were cold. But he knew it was just nerves. He felt it, too. Being with her like this. Talking about old times. Longing to be close again.

"You're welcome." He shut his eyes for just a moment, trying to shut out the vision of her angelic face. But it stayed in his mind, permanently embedded there.

"See you tomorrow night." She stepped toward the door.

"Yeah, see you."

And then she was gone. And he was all alone. Again.

Chapter Eight

The next time she worked the dinner shift at the ranch, Julie was again the last person to leave the dining hall. She liked the quiet solitude after the kids had bustled outside for their fun activities before settling down for Campfire Hour.

She'd quickly learned that mealtimes took a lot of effort at Sunrise Ranch, but she enjoyed the work. She loved her work with the Forest Service, too, but helping at Sunrise Ranch gave her a sense of purpose she hadn't felt before. As if she could really make a difference for a child.

She was wiping down the countertops when Lyn found her in the kitchen. Holding Clarisse in one arm, Lyn gave Julie a hug and thanked her profusely. "I'm so glad you decided to help us out. I can see why Dal thinks so highly of you. What would we do without you?"

Scarlet heat charged up Julie's neck and flooded her face. She felt awkward, not used to a physical show of affection from others. She merely smiled, not knowing what to say. Instead, she tugged playfully on the baby's foot and tickled her tummy. In response, Clarisse chortled and waved her tiny arms. Julie couldn't help wishing she had a little daughter of her own to cherish. She liked the Baldwin family. A lot.

"You've done enough work for tonight," Lyn said. "Come on out to the corrals. You'll want to see Dal's special surprise for the kids."

Lyn waited for Julie to put away the cleanser and toss her soiled dishcloth into the laundry bin. Together they walked outside toward the barn.

"You should come out to the ranch tomorrow morning," Lyn said.

"Why?"

"That's when the kids will start their riding lessons. We take them one at a time. The first one is at seven-fifteen. Afterward, you could go into work. You wouldn't be very late."

"What do you do with the rest of the kids while one of them is riding?" Julie asked.

"They go to the lake for fishing and swimming, or they experience the zip line for the first time. Or they help me in the garden. I let them plant flowers in a pot that they can take home to grow. We've got tons of activities to keep them all busy."

Julie wished she could see some of the kids ride at least once. She was a pretty good equestrian herself and loved horses. Maybe she had time for just one lesson in the morning.

No, she should go for her morning run and then go into work. She was spending too much time out here at the ranch as it was. And she loved being here.

"So what's Dal's special surprise tonight?" Julie asked.

"You'll see. I don't want to spoil it for you. He uses this surprise as a teaching moment for the kids. To motivate them to never, ever give up on themselves."

A sense of urgency built within Julie as she wondered what it could be. Though it was almost eight o'clock in the evening, the summer sun brought longer days and still gleamed bright in the western sky. Lyn and Julie paused at the corrals where the kids had congregated with the staff members. They all stood in a semicircle, as though waiting for something amazing. Curious, Julie stood up on the bottom rail of the fence and wrapped her arms around the top rail to get a better view.

Dal came out of the barn, leading a small roan mare. At first sight, Julie stared, wide-eyed. The horse walked with an uneven gait, caused by the large prosthesis on her right front leg. Like the kids, the horse was an amputee. A hard lump settled in Julie's chest. Compassion overwhelmed her, catching her off guard. She'd never seen a large animal like this with only three legs.

"Here she is," Dal called to the crowd of kids. "This is my big surprise."

A low murmur of oohs and aahs swept over the group. Both kids and adults stared in amazement, but didn't rush the mare. They held back, and Julie thought they must have received some instructions beforehand.

"What's her name?" one of the kids with a crutch tucked beneath his arm asked.

"This is Polly."

"How old is she?" another child asked.

"About three years."

"Can I pet her?" Marcus asked, crowding in close.

Holding the mare's halter, Dal gave the boy a kind look. "Yes, but remember I said you'd have to pet her one at a time." He then spoke to the entire group. "You need to be gentle and try not to spook her. Remember that Polly has a lot in common with each of you. You're all amputees. So treat her the way you'd like to be treated."

Marcus gave a somber nod, his dark eyes round with awe. He stepped close, and that seemed to give the other kids the cue. They lined up close, ready to wait their turns. The adult staff members directed the kids so they each got a chance to touch and admire the mare.

"Everyone will get a turn," Dal said when several kids jostled for position in the line.

Polly stood completely still, head up, ears pricked forward. Her dark eyes showed keen intelligence. She seemed highly alert, but not at all bothered by the barrage of children's laughter and excited voices.

"How'd Polly lose her leg?" Marcus asked after he'd had a turn to stroke the mare's silky mane.

"She was a wild mustang and rounded up when she was about one year old." Dal spoke loud enough for everyone to hear. "They believed she must have been attacked by a mountain lion. Her mangled leg had become infected to the point that she needed to be put down."

A cute girl of perhaps seven years with long brown hair and no arms hopped up and down to get attention. Her brows pinched together in perplexity.

"Jenna, do you have a question?" Dal asked.

"Yes. What does 'put down' mean?"

Marcus shoved one of her arm stumps with his prosthetic hand. "It means they were gonna kill her, stupid."

"Marcus! Be nice." Dal shot him a warning frown.

The boy gave an irritable jerk of his shoulder, a bored expression on his face.

"That's kind of a mean way to say it, but I'm afraid it's true," Dal said. "But when a veterinarian puts an animal down, they usually do it gently, with a shot that makes the animal go to sleep. They don't feel any pain, but they never wake up. It's called euthanasia."

"Why would they do that?" Jenna's bottom lip trembled, her large blue eyes filled with sadness.

"Because they thought the horse was too sick to live. They thought they'd be doing Polly a kindness."

Jenna's voice filled with tears. "You mean they were gonna kill poor Polly?"

Dal smiled and spoke in a gentle tone.

"Yes, but I bought her instead and worked with a local vet to save her leg. When that didn't work, he amputated her leg and I worked to get her to walk on a special-made prosthetic limb provided by Dr. Baldwin."

"Wow, that's amazing," another boy said.

Yes, it certainly was. Julie was stunned by this remarkable story.

"How do you know it wasn't better for Polly to be put down? Now she has to live without one of her legs," Marcus grumbled.

"That Marcus," Lyn murmured for Julie's ears alone.

Julie understood Lyn's frustration. "He's so angry all the time."

"Yes, he's just like Kristen was once upon a time."

"What do you mean?" Julie's gaze sought out Kristen, who now stood behind Jenna, her arms wrapped around the younger girl in a protective gesture.

Lyn shifted the baby to her other hip. "After Kristen's father died in the accident that took her leg, she was angry and belligerent all the time. No matter what I did, I just couldn't get through to her."

Kristen seemed so sweet and affectionate. Julie couldn't imagine the girl acting as cantankerous as Marcus. "What finally changed her?"

Lyn's gaze rested on Cade, who stood among the kids handling crowd control. "A lot of things, actually. First, Cade and I loved her. We refused to give up on her, no matter what. Plus, she had the misconception that it was her fault her daddy had died. We finally had a long talk, and I assured her it wasn't her fault at all. That seemed to change everything for her."

A sharp breath whooshed from Julie's lungs. "Do you think that might be Marcus's problem, too?"

"Who knows? I tried to talk with him about it once, to make sure he knew it wasn't his fault that his parents died, but he shut me out. At least Kristen had me, but Marcus has no one. I hope someone can get through to him soon."

Julie's blood ran cold when she thought

about Marcus's sad situation. How she wished she could help him somehow. He must be craving attention to act so bratty all the time. But she was basically a complete stranger. She doubted he'd let her speak with him. And she hated the thought of his growing up cold and remote as she had. What he really needed was a family to love and care for him.

As Julie watched the kids pet the little horse one by one, she felt overwhelmed by Dal's generosity. This was a great place for Marcus to be, to begin healing from what he'd been through. But what would become of him at the end of the summer when he had to leave?

She knew the answer firsthand. He'd be shuffled from one foster home to another until he had no sense of identity and very little self-worth. From the few statistics she knew, he'd possibly end up in a gang, living on violence, drugs and crime. Unless some special people interceded for him.

Dal's deep laughter filled the air, and she gazed at him with wonder as he patted the horse's neck. Julie could just imagine Polly's plight when she'd first been rounded up. Wild and in a great deal of pain, she was a prime candidate for death. Yet that hadn't stopped Dal. He could have taken the easy route and let the vet euthanize the mustang. Instead, he'd cared for the horse. He'd spent a lot of time helping her and had given her a second chance at life.

"Can I ride her?" Marcus asked, sidling close.

Dal shook his head. "Sorry, bud. Polly's just for petting. She can't support any extra weight on her bad leg." He then addressed all the children. "Whenever you look at Polly, I want you to remember that there's nothing you can't do. Nothing you can't overcome. Nothing you can't try."

Jenna's turn was next. With no hands to pet the mare, the girl cuddled close against the horse's chest. Jenna embraced Polly with her two arm stumps, her face pressed against the animal's warm body. In response, Polly lowered her head down and snuffled at Jenna. The girl rubbed her cheek against Polly's as they breathed each other in. Two kindred spirits.

A burning pressure at the backs of her eyes forced Julie to blink several times. An overwhelming conviction filled her with warmth. That God loved all creatures on earth. Even the sick and the maimed. These children had been hurt, their bodies bruised and broken. Just like the Savior. And yet, Christ had risen from the grave on the third day. Likewise, these kids had futures ahead of them, each and every one. It wouldn't be easy, but Julie knew they all had a mission to perform here on earth. To learn and grow and reach their full potential.

To return to a loving Father in Heaven at the end of their lives.

Swiping at her eyes, Julie looked up and saw Dal talking to Marcus again. The boy listened intently to every word. Julie wondered if perhaps they might actually be able to get through to the sullen boy. Maybe this camp was just what he needed to make a difference in his life.

"Life isn't easy, is it?" Dal spoke to the

kids again. "You each have huge obstacles you'll need to overcome. It's not fair, but you can do it. It won't be easy, but your life has just begun. The rest of this week, we're gonna have a lot of fun activities for you. I hope you'll each participate, even if you're afraid. I want you to push yourselves and take chances. And I promise we'll be here beside you the entire time. There's nothing you can't do. Don't let anyone tell you differently. You just have to want it bad enough to find a way."

Dal's words seeped deep into Julie's soul. Fortifying her. Strengthening her and the morale of each child within hearing distance. The kids' faces glowed with burgeoning optimism. A desire to believe glimmered in their eyes. They wanted to accept what Dal said. To overcome their physical limitations.

They wanted to believe in themselves.

And Marcus. The sullen hostility had faded from his expression, replaced by a flame of hope. For just a moment, Dal's words sank in deep.

But it didn't last long. Another child scooted in to pet Polly and Marcus thrust the boy away. "Get back. You've already had your turn."

"Marcus." Dal cupped his hand around the base of the boy's neck as he spoke in a soothing tone. "Everyone can have as many turns as they like. There are no limits. Not here. If I have to stand out here all night long with each of you, I won't go inside until you've had enough of Polly. Of course, she'll be here again tomorrow, and the next day, too. So you'll all have the opportunity to become good friends with her."

Marcus looked down and kicked at a clod of dirt. "I sure wish I could ride her."

"It's not possible," Dal said. "Imagine if you weren't strong enough, but someone climbed onto your back anyway. It wouldn't be much fun, would it? But don't worry. Tomorrow morning, we're all gonna ride some other horses."

Marcus flashed a wide grin, the first time Julie had seen him smile. And Julie wished she could be here with them. To witness each child learning to ride a horse for the first time. Maybe she could go into work late. Maybe—

"Hooray!" the children cheered with excitement.

Yes, *hooray!* Julie thought. Hooray that these amputee kids had such a wonderful place like Sunrise Ranch to come and play for a while. To forget their troubles. To forget they were different.

Hooray that a kind man like Dallin Savatch lived and walked the earth. And hooray that Julie was so honored to know him.

"Okay, kids. Time for Campfire Hour," Cade called from the corral gate. Seemingly pacified that he'd get to see Polly again later, Marcus headed toward the main yard with the rest of the kids.

"I thought you were already gone for the evening." Surprised to see Julie standing beside the fence, Dal led Polly over to her.

Cade and the other staff directed the kids toward the fire pit. But not until every child had told Dal personally that they were ready to let Polly go inside her warm stall for the night.

"I stuck around to meet Polly." Julie reached through the fence and rubbed the mare's soft muzzle.

"Yeah, she's amazing, isn't she?" He patted the horse's neck.

Julie looked at him, her brown eyes seeing into him, to his very soul. "Remember that filly your mother bought you back when we were still in high school?"

"Yes, I remember." He couldn't resist showing a sad little smile.

"It was all your mom could afford. She knew how much you wanted a horse of your own, so she bought that scruffy little horse and told you to raise it up right. You fed and groomed that horse every day. You started training her right away. You couldn't wait until she was old enough to ride and were so upset when you found out you couldn't ride her until she was about four years old."

He nodded, a barrage of memories flooding his mind. He'd loved that horse and had spent every free minute with her and Julie. "Yes, I named her Candy Dance."

"Whatever happened to Candy?"

"I…I raised her to be a good saddle horse. But I had to sell her when Mom got sick. I used the money to pay the doctor bills."

"Oh. I'm sorry, Dal."

He shrugged, wishing his mom could be here with him now. Wishing he'd been able to keep her and Julie safe. "It was no sacrifice. Not really. We needed the money, and I'd do it again without even thinking twice. No animal is more important than people. Not for me."

"I understand. Nothing is more important than family. Especially to those of us who don't have any. I think we can fully appreciate how great our parents were, because we lost them when we were so young."

He met her gaze. "I wish I had a million horses I could sell to bring Mom back."

"I know. I wish I could bring my parents back, too. You were always such a kind, generous person, Dal. I can't believe what you've done for Polly and what you do for the kids here at Sunrise Ranch. You're such a caring, wonderful man. You always were."

He jerked his hand away from Polly and held the reins in a death grip. "Don't say things like that."

She drew back, an expression of astonishment etching her soft face. "Why not? It's the truth. Why can't I say it?"

"Because I..." Because he loved her, and hearing her say such things only made the distance between them harder for him to bear. "I've got to put Polly to bed. I'll see you tomorrow, okay?"

He tugged on the reins, giving Polly time to turn on her prosthesis and walk with him back toward the barn.

"Good night."

He heard Julie's whispered farewell from behind and could imagine her gaze following him. Boring into him like a high-speed drill.

He didn't look back at her, but he wanted to. He stifled a pang of regret. He was doing the right thing. Wasn't he? He resisted the urge to turn around, forcing himself to stare straight ahead. To focus on Polly and ignore the harsh pounding of his heart. To take slow, even breaths and pretend he didn't care about Julie.

To pretend he didn't love her.

Chapter Nine

The following morning, Julie drove out to Sunrise Ranch and arrived promptly at seven o'clock. As she parked her car in the driveway and got out, she lifted her face to the warmth of the sun. A light breeze blew down from the mountains, carrying the earthy scent of horses and sage.

Looking toward the house, Julie caught sight of Lyn standing on the front porch. Lyn stood hunched over, holding a green watering can. She tilted the spout so that a spray of water cascaded down over numerous clay pots filled with hot pink petunias.

"Hi, Lyn." Julie waved to get the other woman's attention.

"Julie!" Lyn set the watering can on the first step and came down to greet her. "You made it. I wasn't sure you were going to be able to come see the riding lessons. Can you stay long?"

Julie shook her head, gripping a pair of leather riding gloves with her fingers. "No, I've got to go into work. But I thought I'd at least catch the first lesson of the day, just to see how it's done."

Lyn walked with her toward the stables, the blazing sunlight gleaming off her long white-blond ponytail. "I hope you're not disappointed. Marcus has the first lesson."

"Oh?"

"Yeah, we figured maybe if he went first, he'd be more cooperative throughout the rest of the day's activities. That's why Dal's teaching today."

"Dal? I thought it was Cade's turn for riding lessons today."

Lyn flashed a playful smile. "Normally it is, but Marcus seems to respond better to Dal. And Cade's been called away on a medical emergency. A woman went into early labor, so he's riding with her to Elko, just to make sure she gets to the hospital in time before the baby's born. If not, he'll be delivering a baby on the roadside."

Julie cringed at the thought. She didn't understand why, but knowing Dal was giving the riding lessons today made her feel a tad uneasy. She'd expected Cade to be there, but she tried to tell herself it didn't matter. She and Dal were just friends. She couldn't help being highly anxious to see him again, though she told herself it was no big deal.

"Well, have fun." Lyn kept walking toward the garden.

Julie hesitated. "You're not coming in?"

Lyn flashed a quick smile. "No, I've got to get started on lunch. Lots of sandwiches to make. I'll see you tomorrow evening for dinnertime."

The woman disappeared around the corner, and Julie paused in front of the wide double doors of the stable. Taking a deep breath, she stepped inside and blinked to accustom her eyes to the dim interior. An elderly volunteer staff member named Grant was mucking out a stall and nodded a greeting. A bay gelding had been tethered with a halter to the hitching rail. Dal stood with his back toward her, showing Marcus how to curry the horse.

"Rub the currycomb around in small circular motions. See how it loosens up the dirt and sweat in Banjo's coat?" Dal said.

"That's what I'm doing." Marcus bit out the terse reply.

"Good work."

Rather than snapping back, Dal stood silent while the boy shifted from long, weak strokes to tight circles. Although Marcus had not been doing as instructed, he'd made an adjustment without Dal causing a big scene. Once again, Julie was amazed by his insight in dealing with the difficult child. She stood there in the shadows, enjoying their hushed camaraderie. The heavy scent of clean straw and horses filled the air, along with quiet warmth.

The horse shifted its weight, and Dal smiled. "Ah, he likes that, Marcus. You're getting rid of all his itchy spots. Well done."

The child's lips twitched, betraying his urge to smile. But he didn't, and Julie wondered how he could resist.

"So have you ever ridden a horse before?" Dal asked.

"No, of course not."

"What else do you like to do?"

Marcus shrugged.

"Do you like to play ball?" Dal persisted.

Marcus held up the stump of his amputated hand, his face contorted with irritation. "Do I look like I can play ball?"

"Sure you can. You can do anything if you set your mind to it. When are you going to try out the new prosthetic hand Dr. Baldwin fitted you with?"

Marcus turned back toward the horse. "It feels odd. I don't like it."

Julie almost laughed. This boy didn't like anything. It occurred to her that he appeared tough, but it was all an act. On the inside, Marcus was just a scared little boy seeking approval.

She took a step, and Dal looked her way. His eyes widened with surprise, his gaze scouring her forest ranger's uniform. "Hi, Jules. I didn't know you'd be here today."

She moved nearer, her hands in her pants pockets. "I just wanted to watch for an hour. I've got to go into work right after Marcus's lesson ends."

"Okay, you and Grant can help us out."

"You came out here just for my lesson?" Marcus asked.

A feeling of compassion squeezed Julie's heart, and she reached out and rested her hand on his shoulder before she thought to stop herself. "Of course I wanted to see you ride. I wouldn't miss it for the world."

And she meant it. Helping this boy feel special seemed so important to her right now. Without asking permission, she hugged him. A quick, spontaneous action that she didn't stop to think about until it was over with.

Marcus's lips curved in a smile for about two seconds. Then the ugly frown returned, as though he didn't want to show any joy at all.

Julie rubbed the gelding's soft muzzle. The

horse blew dust from its nostrils, breathing in Julie's scent. Otherwise, Banjo stood completely still, seeming to enjoy his rubdown.

"I get to ride first before any of the other kids today," the boy said.

"So I heard," Julie replied with enthusiasm.

"Okay, I think we're ready. Go and get your saddle blanket," Dal urged.

The boy stepped away, and Dal spoke low, for her ears alone. "What are you really doing out here this morning?"

Honestly? She had no idea. "I, um, Lyn suggested I come out at least once, to see the kids ride. I just wanted to know what you did and how you worked with the kids. For the fun of it. I'm glad I'll get to see Marcus ride."

Okay, that was truthful enough. She couldn't betray a feeling of euphoria that she got to see Dal, too. Being near him had become a tonic she couldn't seem to do without. She felt drawn to him and didn't understand why.

He studied her expression for several moments, then gave her a smile. "Good. As usual, we're shorthanded. I'll let you serve as one of the side walkers."

She arched her brows. "Side walker?"

"Yeah, each kid who rides has a horse handler to hold on to the halter, and two side walkers to make sure the child is balanced safely on the horse and doesn't fall off."

"Okay. Sounds easy enough. I'm glad to help." She reached for the saddle sitting on a rack nearby.

Dal interceded, resting his hand on her arm. "Nope, the kids saddle their own horses."

At her confused expression, he explained. "It's good for them to work with the horse and become friends. To learn to trust their mount."

"Here it is," Marcus groused. He held the horse blanket over his good arm, using his wrist stump to keep it from falling to the dirt floor.

"Good job," Dal said. "Now just swing it up onto Banjo's back."

He waited for Marcus to do as he was told. The boy released an irritated huff of air and pursed his lips in disgust. Then he made a weak attempt to toss the blanket over. The moment the boy made an effort to try, Dal helped, ensuring that the blanket didn't slip off.

"Good job, Marcus." Dal tugged the blanket into position. "You want it to sit right over Banjo's withers. Then slide it back just a bit to make sure the hair is lying flat beneath the pad. That way, the saddle won't rub his back sore."

Julie stood quiet, observing Marcus's expressions. The boy listened intently, but the grumpy glare remained.

"Okay, now it's time for the saddle." Dal nodded at the worn leather sitting nearby on a rack, the stirrups shortened to fit a child. He waited for Marcus to reach for it.

"I can't do it." The boy held up his stumped arm, as if it were obvious why he couldn't lift the saddle.

Julie's heart gave a powerful jerk. Compassion overwhelmed her. She wanted to help. To protect this boy from being hurt by the world. To do everything for him. But she waited for Dal, knowing he was the expert in this situation. Knowing Marcus had to learn to be independent if he were to ever have a normal life of his own.

"Sure you can do it." Dal smiled, seemingly oblivious to Marcus's frigid glare. "Just loop your stump through the gullet of the saddle like this. You don't have a hand on that wrist, but you can use the strength of your arm to lift the weight and hold on to the cantle with your other hand."

Dal showed Marcus what to do, then stood back and waited for the boy to try it. Marcus didn't budge. Didn't even flinch. "I said I can't do it."

"Sure you can. At least try it," Dal said.

The boy gave a stubborn shake of his head.

"Okay, no problem. You can try again tomorrow." Dal tugged off the blanket and set it aside.

"Wait! You…you mean I can't ride today?" Marcus wailed.

"Not without a saddle."

"But...but you can saddle Banjo for me."

Dal shook his head. "Sorry, Marcus. Remember, I explained the rules. Everyone has to saddle their own horse, or at least try."

Marcus leaned against a post, his little back and shoulders completely rigid.

Dal showed a look of confusion. "Have I misunderstood you, buddy? Do you still want to ride today?"

Julie remained stone still. From what she could see, it was obvious that Marcus didn't fear the horse. He was simply using a power play to get Dal to saddle the horse for him. Her fingers itched to pick up the saddle and perform this simple chore for Marcus. It would only take a moment. But she resisted the urge to help. She must allow Dal to work with this child. To teach Marcus that he could overcome this obstacle, if he would only try.

"Of course I want to ride." Tears glimmered in the boy's eyes, but he stubbornly kept them from falling.

"Okay," Dal said. "Then saddle your horse. I'll help you if you need me to."

"No! I don't want to saddle Banjo."

"Then who will do it for you?"

"You will." Marcus pointed at Dal's chest.

Again, Dal shook his head, looking very sorry. "I won't always be there with you, Marcus. Banjo needs to trust you. If you can't at least make an attempt to saddle him, how can you ever sit on his back, hold the reins and ride him?"

The boy gazed at the ground and kicked at the dirt as he thought this over. Then an obstinate glint filled his eyes with flashing fire. Stepping over to the rack, Marcus reached for the saddle. He looped his stumped wrist through, beneath the soft fleece lining and grunted as he lifted the leather seat up against Banjo's side. The horse didn't budge, proving he was a patient creature and perfect for being ridden by nervous kids who had never done this before.

The moment the boy made the effort, Dal slid the blanket back onto the horse's back.

Marcus struggled with the heavy leather for only a moment. Then Dal took hold of the cantle with his strong hands and removed the bulk of the weight from Marcus's thin arms. Julie stepped in to help, flipping the stirrups out of the way as Dal helped Marcus settle the saddle into place.

"Well done! See? You can do it." Dal laughed and ruffled the boy's dark hair.

Marcus showed half a smile.

"Now let's tighten the cinch. Loop it through here." Dal pointed, then waited for Marcus to do the work. When he struggled with the strips of leather, Dal helped. But not until Marcus had at least made an effort.

"Now comes the tricky part. Wait for Banjo to exhale before you tighten it up." Dal paused. The moment Banjo released his breath, Dal tugged the cinch tight.

Marcus tilted his head, his eyes wide with curiosity. "Why did you do that?"

"So we can get the saddle on tight enough. Banjo is a clever horse. He knows that if he holds his breath when you're saddling him, it'll make the saddle looser around his middle and more comfortable for him. But it's not as safe for you. The saddle will be too wobbly. So if you wait a moment, you can tighten it up."

Marcus laughed and patted Banjo's neck. "Clever horse. But we outwitted you."

Julie's mouth dropped. This was the first time she'd heard the boy laugh. Over Marcus's head, her gaze met Dal's and they shared a conspiratorial smile. They'd made progress today. Not only had Dal gotten Marcus to make an effort, but the boy had also laughed. Julie couldn't believe Dal's patience, even when the boy was so irritable. Dal seemed to know just how far he could push the boy before he needed to let up.

Reaching down, Dal handed the reins to Marcus. "Lead your horse outside to the hitching rail so you can mount up."

Marcus took hold of the reins with his good hand and headed out. His forehead kneaded with a bit of uncertainty, until the horse followed after him at a slow walk. Julie noticed that Dal held on to the halter, never fully relinquishing control over the animal. At this point in Marcus's riding education, it wouldn't be safe. Even a calm animal like Banjo could hurt the young boy.

Quietly observing their exchange, Grant followed them outside into the sunshine. Julie hurried ahead and reached for the step stool, sliding it into place. Marcus stood up on it without being asked. Finally. Finally the boy seemed to be in sync with them.

Dal showed him how to place his left foot into the stirrup, loop the elbow joint of his amputated hand around the saddle horn and pull himself on board.

When he was seated, Marcus held the reins in his good hand. For several moments, the boy just sat there, blinking in surprise, as though he couldn't believe he was actually sitting on a horse. Grant snapped a quick picture as Marcus whooped with glee. "Hey, I'm on. I did it. I really did it."

"You sure did." Julie clapped her hands together while Dal chuckled.

"Very well done, Marcus," Dal praised. "You brushed and saddled your own horse. I can see that Banjo trusts you by the way he's calmly waiting for your commands. You've done a good job today and have earned a fun ride."

A look of pure bliss settled across Marcus's face. He absorbed Dal's compliments like dry sand soaking up sunshine.

"Come on, Banjo. Let's go." Marcus flicked the reins, but the horse didn't budge.

"Tell him to 'walk on.' You'll need to tap your heels gently against Banjo's sides, the way I taught you," Dal said. "Not too hard, but hard enough to get his attention. Remember to treat your horse with kindness, and he'll always trust you. If you treat him with cruelty, you'll never have good luck with him. Horses are just like people. They respond to kindness." Dal took hold of the halter lead and nodded at Julie.

She pushed the step stool out of the way and took up her position on the left side of the horse, while Grant stood on the right side.

"Walk on." Marcus tapped his heels against Banjo's flanks and the horse walked forward, nice and slow.

With Dal leading the gelding, they moved out into the corral. A bit of nervous energy flickered in Marcus's eyes, but he soon became comfortable, rocking gently with the gait of the horse.

"Your seat is very good. Great conformation," Julie praised the boy. "You sure don't need much help. You can do it all by yourself."

"Yeah, I'm a good rider," Marcus said. A smile widened his face as he gave himself over completely to the horse.

For half an hour, they walked and trotted the horse. And Julie laughed and praised each and every one of Marcus's accomplishments.

On their way back to the stable, Dal reached down and plucked a yellow plume of goldenrod growing among the tall grass at the base of the fence. He promptly handed it to Julie.

Her eyes met his and, though he didn't say a word, his gaze spoke volumes. The gesture caused her heart to beat faster and her head to spin.

* * *

The moment he gave Julie the flower, Dal regretted it. It had been an automatic gesture. He'd seen a flower and given it to a beautiful girl.

His beautiful girl.

Except she wasn't. His anyway. Not anymore.

Looking away, he tried to focus on Marcus and the horse. After Dal helped Marcus step off the horse, Grant led the gelding back inside the stable where Marcus more willingly assisted in unsaddling his mount.

"I wish I could ride a little longer," Marcus said.

Not a demand. No pouting. Just a quick comment as the boy slid the blanket off Banjo's back. Yes, they had definitely made a lot of headway with the child. And Dal was abundantly grateful that he'd gotten to share today's accomplishment with Julie.

"Don't worry. You'll get to ride again tomorrow morning," Dal said.

"Yes!" The boy fisted his hand in the air and gave a happy little hop.

The next student hobbled into the stable, accompanied by another staff member. An eleven-year-old boy with a double above-the-knee amputation, he used a walker to support his shuffling limp.

"Hi, Tony. I'll be right with you." Dal spoke over his shoulder to the boy.

"How was your ride?" Tony asked Marcus, a tone of wary eagerness in his voice.

"Great! You're gonna love it. It's so easy, and Banjo is a great horse," Marcus replied.

Dal's mouth dropped open, and he couldn't help staring. This was the first time he'd heard Marcus speak civilly to one of the other kids. It reaffirmed the therapeutic value of having the kids interact with and ride the horses.

Julie mirrored his surprise, looking between him and the children. Then she closed her mouth and smiled. "Well, I'd better get going. My office manager will wonder what happened to me."

She looked at Dal. "Do you have someone else to work as a side walker without me here?"

"Yes, we'll be fine." He said the words, but he didn't mean them. Not really. He couldn't help wishing that she could stay. But maybe it was better if she left. No matter how hard he tried not to, he'd become overly attached to the pretty forest ranger. And he couldn't help feeling grateful that she'd taken time out of her busy schedule to come here and work with him.

"Goodbye." She gave Marcus another quick squeeze, and he actually hugged her back.

"Do you have to go?" the boy said.

"I'm afraid so. But I'll be back to help serve dinner tomorrow night."

A pleased smile lit up the child's face. "Okay. See you then."

He turned to Tony and started a detailed dialogue on how to groom Banjo and cinch up the saddle.

With a small laugh, Julie waved at Dal. His gaze focused on the soft smile curving her pretty mouth.

He lifted a hand in farewell and watched the graceful swing of her hips as she headed for the doors. Not until Tony tugged on his sleeve did he realize he was staring at empty space. With a gargantuan effort, Dal focused on the boy and vowed to forget about Julie. At least for the next few minutes.

"Okay, Tony. Let's ride a horse."

Chapter Ten

Late Saturday afternoon, Julie lifted the lid of the washing machine and coiled her bed sheets around the drum. Turning the knob, she set the cycle. The rush of water began to fill the machine as she measured out the detergent. A little bit of color-safe bleach, some fabric softener and then she'd finish washing her dishes. She should have just enough time to go into town to buy groceries to fill her empty refrigerator. Then she could relax and watch the evening news. Maybe she'd pick up a take-and-bake pizza for dinner.

The phone rang, and she closed the lid of the washer before answering.

"Hello."

"Julie?"

"Hi, Cade! What's up?" She recognized the doctor's voice immediately, wondering why he would call her on the weekend. They didn't have another batch of kids coming in until Monday morning, and she wasn't scheduled to work until that night.

"Can you come over to the ranch, please?"

She hesitated. "Sure, when?"

"Right now."

She glanced down at her knee-length shorts and bare feet, then at the kitchen clock. Four forty-five in the afternoon. Good thing she hadn't run to the store yet. Groceries and pizza would have to wait.

"Um, okay. What's up?"

He took a deep breath, and she heard the restlessness in his tone. "It's Dal. He needs you. Badly."

"Dal? What's wrong?"

And why hadn't Dal called?

"He received a letter today. Some very bad news. He's kept to himself all day and seems inconsolable."

"A letter from whom?"

"An old friend. He won't confide in me about it. He's been locked away in his cabin all day. He hasn't come out even to eat, and he won't let me come in, either. I haven't seen him like this since…since he lost his leg in the war. I'm worried about him, Julie."

Yeah, she was, too. This wasn't like Dal. Not at all.

"But why call me?" she asked.

"I think you can help. You have a calming influence on him."

She did? That was an interesting observation. She doubted that going over to his place and asking him personal questions about a letter he'd received would help.

"I don't think this is a good idea, Cade. Can't you talk to him?"

"I've tried. So has Lyn. He's shut us both out. But he can never refuse you. I think he'll let you in."

His words impacted her like hitting a wall of cement. *Dal could never refuse her.* She sensed that was true, though she'd never put it to the test. Not really.

She didn't know what to say. Her promise to never abandon Dal again came back to haunt her. He needed her, and she had to go to him. It was that simple.

"I'll be there in twenty minutes." She hung up the handset and made a mad dash for her tennis shoes. The dishes in the kitchen sink, the clean laundry waiting to be folded, the evening news would all have to wait.

Exactly fourteen minutes later, she pulled up in front of Sunrise Ranch. With a quick twist of her wrist, she parked her car, killed the ignition and pushed the door wide-open as she got out.

Cade and Lyn came out onto the white wraparound porch to greet her. Lyn stood beside the swing, holding little Clarisse while Cade pounded down the steps. From their morose expressions, Julie could tell they were very upset.

"Thanks for coming. I didn't know who else to call." Cade spoke in a rush.

Since he was a medical doctor, Julie figured he truly was at wit's end. But what news could have caused Dal this much angst?

Marcus bolted outside and would have run down the porch, but Lyn caught his arm and pulled him back.

"But I want to go with Cade. I want to go see Dal," the boy cried.

"Not right now, buddy. But you'll see him just as soon as possible. I promise," Julie reassured the child.

Marcus sniffed and wiped his nose on his sleeve. For once, he didn't fight them, seeming to understand the gravity of the situation. And that was when Julie realized Marcus had become truly attached to Dal.

Cade directed Julie to the back of the complex, toward the staff cabins. They walked side by side, with Julie lengthening her stride to keep up. Past the gazebo, the fire pit and the volleyball court. Through the tall cottonwoods outlining the perimeter of the ranch.

"Where is he?" In all this time, she'd never been to the staff cabins. Never seen where Dal lived and spent his time when he wasn't working with the horses and kids.

Cade pointed at the largest cabin on the

farthest end. Big enough for a private room and bath, but little more. Not a real house. Not a place anyone would want to live long term. Poor Dal had lived here for several years now.

Not much of a home.

"He's said nothing to you about the letter he received?" she asked.

Cade gave a solemn shake of his head. "Just that it was from a friend with some very sad news."

"Has he… Has he been yelling or throwing things inside his cabin?"

"No, Dal's never been a violent man. He hasn't said a word."

A dark foreboding blanketed her heart. Dal had no family anymore. So what news could be bad enough that he'd sequester himself away like this? "Are you sure he's okay?"

The thought of Dal needing medical attention tore her heart to shreds, and she picked up her pace.

"Physically, he's fine," Cade said. "I've

kept an eye on him all day. I peer inside his window from time to time."

She blinked. "You mean he's just sitting in there? All day long, by himself?"

"Yeah, he hasn't moved since nine o'clock this morning when I brought him the mail. He didn't even go check on the horses. I fed them myself. That's never happened before. He always checks on the animals, no matter what."

Oh, dear. What had happened? When she faced the prospect of questioning Dal, she lost all her courage. An urge to run overwhelmed her, but she resisted with an iron will. Dal needed her. "I can't do this, Cade. You're the doctor, not me."

"Just speak to him," Cade said. "Please. He doesn't want me."

He gazed at her with pleading in his eyes. As she approached the door, Julie had no idea what to expect. No idea what was wrong. No idea how she could help.

She glanced over her shoulder, feeling a little frightened and unsure, drawing reassurance from Cade's presence. He stood beneath the canopy of cottonwoods, his hands in his pockets, a tight smile of encouragement on his lips.

Looking down, Julie noticed a large clay pot of bright pink petunias outside Dal's isolated cabin. How lovely and simple. A mask for the anguish that lay on the other side of the door.

She knocked and waited.

Nothing. No response.

She knocked again, harder this time. Leaning her face close to the rough wood panel, she spoke gently, but loud enough for Dal to hear. "Dal? It's Julie. Can I come in, please? I really need to speak with you."

The silence lengthened. Then a shuffling sound came from inside, followed by the click of the lock, and the door opened just a crack. Through the slit, Julie saw Dal step aside and drop back onto a worn recliner. Determined not to fail, Julie gripped the doorknob and stepped inside, closing the door behind her.

In the dim interior, Dal sat forward in his chair. He rested his elbows on his knees, his hands cupping his face as his fingers threaded through his short hair.

The two-room cabin looked meticulously tidy, with a desk along one wall, a twin-size bed on the other, a love seat and small TV on a table near the entrance. Dark curtains hung across the two windows to keep the sun out. A cloying sadness filled the entire room with gloom.

A shudder swept Dal's body. Julie went to him, going down on her haunches beside him as she rested one hand on his arm. She gazed up at his face, trying to get him to focus on her. "Dal, are you okay?"

He took a tremulous breath, his eyes centered on the coffee table in front of him, his shoulders tensed. The shattered look in his eyes spoke volumes. And that was when Julie saw the letter. Just lying there, the top seam torn open.

Confusion raced through her mind. She changed position, sitting on the table facing him, her head level with his, mere inches away.

"Dal, what's happened? What's wrong?" she tried again.

He sat back and shook his head, refusing to look at her. Grief emanated from every pore of his body. His eyes looked cold and empty.

Defeated.

"I want to help," she said. "I'm not leaving until I get some answers, so you might as well tell me what's going on."

He met her gaze, openly assessing her. "You shouldn't have come here. Did Cade call you?"

His words came out in a hoarse croak, as though he'd been crying or screaming. Maybe both.

"Yes, we're all worried about you. What's happened?"

He blinked his eyes with misery. His hand visibly shook as he pointed at the envelope, but he didn't speak.

The envelope crinkled as she picked it up and noted the return address—a Doris Hadley in Texas. "May I read it?"

At his subtle nod, she opened the letter

and scanned the pages. The words poured into her mind. Her head buzzed, and her stomach clenched. Halfway through, a gasp tore from her throat and she pressed trembling fingers to her lips. By the time she finished, she was heartsick. Now she knew what was troubling Dal. And she realized he had every reason to be upset.

In slow movements, she tucked the letter back inside its envelope and placed it on the table. Her mind raced as she thought about what she should say. For the first time in a long time, she prayed for help.

Reaching out, she rested her hands on Dal's knees, willing him to meet her gaze. He did, his features harsh.

"Quinn Hadley was a friend of yours?"

Dal nodded.

"A good friend?"

Another nod.

"And Doris is his mother?"

"Yes." An emotional croak.

"Were you in the war with Quinn?"

"No. We met at the veterans' hospital, after…after we both lost our legs."

"Ah, I see. Quinn was an amputee, too?"

"Yes, he lost his leg up to the hip and also his right forearm. His wife divorced him six months ago. She couldn't accept him anymore. She got tired of being with him, and it broke his heart."

Julie clenched her eyes closed, fighting off the pain his words caused her. Fighting to find the right words to ease his anguish.

"I…I thought he was doing so much better," Dal said. "He'd moved in with his mom. But then he stopped writing. I hadn't heard from him in eight weeks. I don't have a computer out here, so we didn't send email. We both kind of liked using the U.S. Mail instead. No one answered the phone when I tried to call him last week. I figured maybe they'd gone on vacation. Then I got the letter from Doris today."

"I'm so sorry, Dal. So very sorry."

Dal choked out a harsh laugh. "Quinn always had more courage than me. He finally did what I didn't have the guts to do so long ago."

Julie released a shuddering breath. "No,

you're wrong, Dal. You're the most courageous man I know. It takes a lot of guts to keep on living after what you've been through. Living and working every day. Serving others the way you do. Never giving up. That's real courage."

"Well, Quinn is home now. He's free," Dal said. "But I don't know if I should rejoice for him or cry for him."

Tears burned the backs of Julie's eyes. But Dal didn't cry, and she thought it might help if he did.

Suicide. A ghastly option for people who had given up all hope. Quinn had taken his own life. Something Julie had once thought of doing herself, before her social worker had pulled her out of a horrible foster home and sent her to live with Berta Alvey. In retrospect, Julie was so grateful she'd chosen to keep living. But her heart ached for those people who chose not to keep going.

"And what about you?" she asked.

He licked his lips. "What do you mean?"

She inclined her head toward the letter. "Would you ever take your own life?"

She held her breath, fearing the worst. Fearing she might have to get Cade in here with a straitjacket to haul Dal off to a mental hospital. No matter what, she was not leaving Dal alone until she was certain he was okay.

He snorted. "I'd be a liar if I said I hadn't thought about it back when I first lost my leg. But that was a long, long time ago, Julie."

Her throat tightened and her face grew hot. "And what about now?"

His gaze locked with hers. In his eyes, she saw complete conviction.

"No. I feel terrible about Quinn taking his own life, but that's not for me." He reached out and cupped her cheek with his hand, looking deep into her eyes. "Were you afraid for me?"

She nodded.

He gave her a comforting smile. "No need, sweetheart. I'm fine. I'm not done living yet. I'm just mourning the death of a good friend."

"I'm glad to hear that."

He sat back and gazed at the letter. "I was in shock, finding out the way I did. This hit a little too close to home. I needed to take the day to grieve. I'm not sure why, but I know God hasn't abandoned me. He never did, even at my darkest moment. I can't see it yet, but I believe the Lord has my life all figured out, if I can just have faith and endure to the end."

A breath of relief rushed past her lips, and she smiled. "I think maybe you've been alone too long today. It's time to move on now."

"Yeah, you're right. I'm sorry I frightened you." He reached out and brushed his fingertips against her arm. A soft gesture that sent warmth radiating throughout her entire body.

"I'm just glad you're okay," she said.

"Me, too. And I'm starving."

She laughed. "I'm so glad to hear that."

But now she had an even greater problem on her hands. She never should have started working at Sunrise Ranch. Never should have gone jogging with Dal or ever seen him again. Never should have agreed to come out to the ranch today. Because now, whether she liked it or not, she was irrevocably in love with Dal. And that scared her most of all.

Dal gazed into Julie's eyes. He saw the fear etching her face. The concern for him. He hated for her to see him like this. Hurting. Brokenhearted. Bereft. She had enough problems of her own without having to deal with his troubles, too.

"Thanks for worrying about me, Julie. There are a lot of men who come home from the war pretty torn up. But you need to know suicide was never for me." He spoke the words with conviction. Meaning them with every fiber of his being.

"I'm so glad to hear that, Dal. I…I don't know what I'd do if I lost you again."

Her words shredded his heart. What little he had left. If only they'd met again before he'd gone off to war. Before he'd lost his leg and given up on love and marriage.

"Is Cade outside?" He jutted his chin toward the closed door, knowing Cade must be there waiting for them. Hovering around the cabin like a mother grizzly bear.

"Yes, both he and Lyn were afraid for you. They didn't know what to do, so they called me. Even Marcus is worried. You have a lot of people who care about you, Dal."

Of course she cared about him. A pathetic amputee whom she feared might be on the edge of taking his own life. But the last thing he could accept from her now was pity. He wanted her to look at him as a man, whole and complete. Strong and virile. Attractive and masculine. Not as someone she felt sorry for.

"I appreciate your concern."

But he wanted so much more. Why had God spared his life only to let him live as a lonely man like this? Yes, Dal had friends. He had a great job that made a difference for lots of amputee kids who had many struggles facing them throughout their lives. Dal loved his work, but he wanted more.

If only God could take this longing from him, Dal would be a happy man. In all these long, lonely years, he'd never lost his desire for marriage and a family to love. And since Julie had entered his life again, that longing had increased, blazing inside him like an inferno.

He braced his hands on the armrests of his chair, set his feet beneath him and stood. "I think it's time I left this dingy cabin. I'm starving."

"I'm so glad to hear that." She stood also, a soft smile creasing her lips.

"It hasn't been easy, you know?"

"What?"

"Seeing you again. Being near you."

She looked away. "I know."

So many words were left unsaid between them. So many emotions waged war inside his heart.

"Come on." She walked to the door, opened it and called for Cade.

Dal waited for his best friend to appear. Cade stood in the doorway, his face drained of color, looking ashen in the growing darkness of twilight. Dal flipped on an overhead light.

"You didn't have to worry about me," Dal told Cade. "I just needed time to mourn by myself for a while."

"Mourn who?" Cade asked.

Dal walked with them to the main house while Julie told Cade about Mrs. Hadley's letter.

"I guess I never knew Quinn Hadley," Cade said.

"No, he came into the veterans' hospital right after me," Dal said. "We went through a lot of pain and rehabilitation together. I should have introduced you to him during the many times you came to visit me, but he didn't want to see anyone for a very long time. Not even his own mother. I'm sorry now that I lost that chance. You would have liked him."

"I'm sure I would have." Cade paused and embraced Dal with one arm. "I'm glad I haven't lost you, pal. Next to my wife, you're my best friend. You were there for me when I needed you the most."

"Likewise, brother." Dal didn't know what else to say.

Inside the main house, Lyn hugged Dal tight and wiped the tears from her eyes. Kristen threw her arms around his waist. Marcus stayed close beside him, quiet and withdrawn. Like most kids, they didn't understand all that was going on, but they knew Dal was in pain and they wanted to comfort him somehow. They all sat in the living room while he told the kids what had happened and that he'd been mourning the death of a dear friend. Marcus didn't speak, his face stoic. And Dal took that opportunity to express his love for life and God. He figured children ought to hear that now and then from the adults in their life. It meant something. It was important. Everyone cried, and Dal felt blessed to have such wonderful people around him.

Marcus sat off by himself, looking grouchy and sullen. They'd made a lot of progress with the boy, but they weren't fully there yet. Dal wasn't sure what might get through to the boy and hoped by the end of the summer he was happier. He didn't want to ever receive a letter from someone telling him that Marcus had committed suicide, as Quinn had. But how could he get through to the boy? What words could he say that might make a major difference? At this point, Dal didn't know.

Starting tomorrow, he'd make a change in their work schedules. He wasn't sure how, but he'd insist that Cade or one of the other staff members work with Julie in the kitchen. Dal would tend Clarisse while Lyn or Cade helped serve the meals to the kids. Anything to put more distance between him and the girl from his past.

Anything to keep from falling more deeply in love with Julie than he already was.

Chapter Eleven

Dal didn't work with Julie in the kitchen the following week. Lyn told her they'd needed to make some changes in job assignments. Julie understood, but doubt niggled at the back of her mind. She couldn't help wondering if Dal had done this because of her. To put some distance between them.

Julie soon got very good at opening the industrial-size cans of soup, tossing large bags of salad and even baking the preformed balls of bread dough to perfection. She enjoyed her work at the ranch, but she missed Dal. Missed his mischievous smile when he snapped his towel at her as she walked past him. Missed helping him scoop out ice cream for their evening chats together.

Tonight, she finished washing down the kitchen countertops before walking outside toward her car. The kids had gathered over at the gazebo, painting porcelain bowls to take home with them on Friday. Frantic screams erupted from the area by the worktables. Without thinking twice, Julie ran in that direction. Two other staff members responded, as well. A group of kids stood clustered together, their arms waving wildly as they beat up on another child. Dal turned from one of the tables, holding a paintbrush in one hand, wearing a red plastic apron over his chest and legs.

"Hey! Break it up," he called, swinging his prosthetic leg around so he could stand up and stop the fight.

Julie helped the other adults pull the kids away. Marcus lay curled on the cement floor, his arms raised over his head to protect his face from the angry blows. His artificial hand had come off in the struggle and lay beside him, a chilling sight in the early evening sunlight. But these kids needed someone to love them in spite of their handicaps, and Julie didn't shy away as she picked it up so it wouldn't get trampled.

A little girl stood sobbing loudly as she held the shattered remnants of her bowl between her left hand and the stump of her right arm. In a glance, Julie could guess what had happened. Cade had told her earlier in the kitchen that Marcus seemed to be backsliding. He kept causing fights and refused to do anything they asked. No one liked him, and Dal had almost given up hope of getting through to him. Not even Kristen seemed to be able to make him behave.

"What's going on here?" Dal asked. "I turn my back for five seconds and bedlam erupts. What happened?"

As Marcus sat up, one of the other boys snatched the prosthetic hand away from Julie and threw it hard at Marcus. "He keeps ruining our art projects. We're sick of him."

Dal held up an arm, speaking in a calming

voice. "Don't do that, Robbie. Two wrongs don't make a right."

"But he won't stop," another girl whined. "We even asked him nicely many times."

"And l-look what he did to my bowl." The first girl held up the broken pieces, sniffing back another sob.

Dal helped Marcus stand, a deep frown creasing his brow. "Is this true, Marcus? Did you break Susan's bowl?"

Marcus glared his response, a trickle of blood running from his nose. Obviously, the kids had reached the breaking point and decided to take matters into their own hands.

Marcus didn't respond. His eyes filled with hate as he glowered at each child. He yanked his arm out of Dal's grasp and stepped away.

Isolated and alone.

"Go on, Marcus. We don't want you here," Robbie yelled as he took a step on his two prosthetic legs. "You're barely even an amputee, just missing your hand. You don't know what it's like to be a real amputee.

You're just a spoiled, rotten kid. No one wants you. Go away!"

"Robbie, that's enough," Dal growled. "I want Marcus. I don't want him to go away. Now apologize to each other."

Marcus's eyes widened, his face going very pale. Without a word, he bulldozed his way through the wall of children and raced toward the stable. Dal called after him, but he kept going.

Setting his paintbrush on the table, Dal shook his head at Robbie. "You shouldn't have said that, Robbie. No matter what, we never throw our people away."

Robbie jutted his chin. "Well, it's true. We don't want him here."

Dal shook his head, his lips tight with disapproval as he looked at all the kids. "You don't understand. Marcus is alone. His parents were both killed in a plane crash. At the end of this summer, he's going back to foster care. Though all of you are amputees, you still have your moms and dads waiting at home for you. People who love and care for you. But Marcus has no one. He's all alone in this world. So maybe you all could have a little compassion for him and try to make friends."

Julie had heard enough. Dal's words burrowed deep within her soul. *No matter what, we never throw our people away.* And she couldn't help thinking that included her. If anyone understood Marcus's predicament, she did. She remembered the empty feeling of abandonment after her parents had died. The feelings of inadequacy. As if she didn't belong anywhere. No one wanted her. She was a problem. A burden. And even Dal's gentle words and deeds couldn't soothe her aching heart. That was how Marcus was feeling right now. She knew it with absolute clarity. And she had to do something about it.

Right now.

Turning, she walked to the stables, looking for Marcus. Dusk lit up the western sky with fingers of pink and gold. Stepping inside, she gazed through the musty shadows, breathing in the heavy scent of hay and horses.

Where could he be?

She walked the line of animal stalls, peering inside each one. The mustangs gazed back at her, snorting, swishing their tails as she passed by.

At the last stall, she stopped. Polly lay inside, nestled down for the night in a bed of clean straw. Marcus was curled up beside her, his eyes filled with angry defiance.

"Marcus." Julie spoke his name softly, gently.

"Go away." He buried his face against the horse.

"I will in just a minute. But first, I want to talk to you. You don't need to say or do anything. Just listen."

Julie opened the gate to the stall and stepped inside. She sat nearby in the straw, bracing her back against the rough wooden wall.

"I was just like you once," she said.

The boy didn't move.

"My parents both died when I was fifteen years old," she continued.

Still not a word from the boy, but his shoulders seemed to shift slightly.

"I was older than you are, but I still thought my world had ended. I was sent away to foster care. I had to leave the boy I loved and all of my friends. My family was gone. I lived with strangers I didn't think wanted me. Not really. I didn't belong. Not anywhere."

He lifted his head just a bit and peered at her with dark, tearful eyes. "How'd they die?"

His words sounded muffled and vague, but she heard them.

"In a terrible car crash. The police told me they hit a deer that went up through the windshield. I don't know more than that. Just that the car went off the road, rolled several times, and they both died instantly."

Marcus sniffed, speaking in a biting tone, tinged by the threat of tears. "Mine died in a plane crash. Something was wrong with the engine. Daddy tried to emergency-land us, but we still crashed. I don't remember what happened after that. I woke up in the hospital. They took my hand, and Mom and Daddy were both dead."

She nodded, her own eyes welling up with tears. "I know. And I'm so very sorry, sweetheart."

"They're not coming back, are they?"

"No, honey. They can't. But I have no doubt they wished that they could. I hate that you have to go through this. I wish so much that I could give you your parents back."

He coughed, as though he couldn't breathe around a lump in his throat. "What did you do when your mom and dad died?"

She licked her bottom lip, trying to gather her courage. "I kept living. That's all any of us can do. I didn't want to, at first. Things went from bad to worse. I had a foster dad who treated me real bad. I hated everyone, including myself."

Her throat constricted, and she was forced to take a deep breath. She feared she might be saying too much, but then decided Marcus needed honesty right now. Not speaking the words wouldn't clear his troubled mind or make his problems go away. Like her, he needed the truth. She hadn't spoken about this in years, to anyone. Not even Berta. And yet, uttering the words seemed to cleanse her soul. To set her free. The abuse was behind her. She could let it go now.

"What happened to you?" Marcus gazed at her with wide, sympathetic eyes.

"My social worker found out about it and moved me. I went to live with a kind woman who loved and raised me as her own. I'll never forget my real mom and dad, but I love Berta so much. She became my mother. There are good people out there, Marcus. People who want you."

"Not me." He shook his head, his eyes filled with disbelief and defeat. "No one wants me. They all hate me."

"If that were true, the people here at Sunrise Ranch would have sent you away long ago. Dal, Lyn, Cade and me. We all want to be friends with you. We want to help. Don't you think you ought to at least give us the benefit of the doubt? I mean, what can it hurt to give us all a chance?"

He looked at her, his thick eyelashes spiked by tears. "I'm s-scared."

And then he broke down. His shoulders shook with deep, gut-wrenching sobs. His tears tore at her heart, and she couldn't stay away any longer. She scooted in close, pulling him into her arms. Rocking him gently as his weeping and Polly's deep breaths filled the air around her.

With his face buried against her shoulder, Marcus murmured his woes to her. Fear that no one would ever want him. That he might have trouble in school and no one would help him with his homework. Or come watch him play football, if he could even throw the ball. Or make him eat all his vegetables.

Fear that he'd never see his parents again.

"Of course you'll see them again, honey." She brushed a hand over his dark hair in soothing strokes.

He took a hiccupping breath. "How do you know?"

"Because I don't believe God would take our parents away from us forever. He loves us too much. We'll see them again. I have faith in this. I believe it to be true."

"I was bad the day they died," he said. "I didn't take the garbage out like Dad asked me to. And it started stinking, so Mom got angry at me. We yelled at each other. I never got to say I was sorry or that I loved them."

"They know. Just like you know they loved you."

Yes, she understood these feelings. The guilt a child felt because their parents had died and they thought it was their fault. For the longest time, Julie had blamed herself. No one had told her any different. That it wasn't her doing.

It just happened.

"You didn't do anything wrong, Marcus. It wasn't your fault that your parents died. I know they'd be here with you if they had a choice. Surely you know that deep inside. And I have no doubt your mom would tell you it's okay to be scared. This is all new to you. But everything is going to be all right. Just trust in God, and you'll be fine."

And saying the words out loud brought Julie a measure of comfort, too. For the first time in a long time, she believed what she said. That God loved her. That He had a plan for her life. That He hadn't abandoned her.

A subtle sound came from the gate, and she looked up. Dal stood there watching her, an intense expression on his face. Listening to every word.

But somehow, she didn't mind. Not anymore.

Dal hadn't meant to intrude. He didn't mean to eavesdrop. But he'd heard a lot. And now he knew the truth. He gritted his teeth when he thought about what the foster dad had done to Julie. His mind went crazy thinking about all the possibilities. Verbal, physical or sexual abuse. If Dal had known, he might have killed the guy. He just hoped the social worker had ensured the man was prosecuted to the fullest extent of the law.

Listening to Julie comfort Marcus did something to Dal deep inside. Her natural motherly instincts touched him as nothing else could. Her gentle reassurance that everything would be okay. That God loved them.

Marcus deserved a sweet mother like Julie. Every kid did.

The boy looked up at Dal and sniffled, his nose red and dripping. "I… I'm sorry, Dal. I wasn't very nice to the other kids. And I'm awful sorry."

Dal lifted the latch to the gate and stepped inside. "Hey, that's okay, pardner."

Julie released the boy, letting him sit up. She searched her pocket for a clean tissue and handed it to him. Marcus blew his nose and wiped his face.

"You feel like coming outside for Campfire Hour now?" Dal asked.

Marcus lifted his brows in a half smile. "Are we roasting marshmallows again?"

Dal nodded. "Every night, you know that. It's a Sunrise Ranch tradition."

Marcus gave a vague smile. Both Julie

and the boy stood, but Julie kept hold of his hand. Marcus looked down at the bed of straw, pursing his lips together in bewilderment. "I guess the kids are pretty mad at me, huh?"

Dal ran a hand through the child's thick hair. "I think they'll forgive you soon enough, if you apologize. And on Monday morning, we get a whole new batch of kids who've never met you before. It's a chance to start fresh and make new friends, don't you think?"

A light gleamed in Marcus's eyes. "That's right. I can start over, can't I?"

"Of course, you can," Julie said. "It's never too late, sweetheart. Because we'll never give up on you. Not ever."

"Even if I do bad things? I may not always be good."

She laughed, and Dal thought she was the most beautiful woman in the world. Gracious, kind and loving.

"Yes, even if you do bad things, we'll be right here for you," she said.

"That's right," Dal said. "You can come

back to Sunrise Ranch every summer, if you like."

Dal wondered if that would be enough. Marcus needed so much more. He needed what all of them needed. A family to love him. A place to belong each and every day.

"Come on," Dal said. "Let's go outside. After you apologize, I'm sure the other kids will want to do the same."

Marcus nodded and took a step. While Julie held the boy's right hand, Dal took hold of Marcus's stump. The scarred skin felt soft and warm to his touch. Dal didn't mind. He was an amputee, too. And this was his purpose at Sunrise Ranch. To help kids like Marcus. To show them that they still had so much to offer the world.

That their scars didn't bother him at all.

As they walked outside, Dal noticed that the tall mercury lights had been turned on. He could see the flickering flames over by the fire pit and the crowd of children as they prepared their s'mores, laughed and talked about the next day's activities. And in that moment, walking side by side with Julie and

Marcus, Dal felt beyond grateful that she'd been here tonight. With all the doctors, specialists and staff members here at the ranch, it had taken a tender forest ranger to finally get through to Marcus.

A feeling of relief blanketed Dal. The conviction that they'd done something good for Marcus tonight and that the boy would be all right. After all, that was what Dal was here for. To make a difference for others. To help in any way he could.

So why did he still feel empty inside? Why did he feel as though life should hold so much more for him?

Chapter Twelve

"I vote we leave Gilway Trail just like it is. It don't need no changes, and we don't want a bunch of handicapped kids riding up there anyway."

Dal froze in his seat. Sitting inside the civic center in town, the blast from the air conditioner did little to cool his steaming face. He was stunned and angry.

Speechless.

"We're not taking a vote, Mr. Watson. This meeting is merely to discuss the proposed changes and voice your concerns." Julie stood before a dry-erase board at the front of the room, her eyes narrowed on Owen Watson, a grizzled old rancher.

Dressed in her Forest Service uniform, she choked an eraser in her right hand, doing an admirable job of controlling her temper.

"Most of them act like retards, the way they hobble around town and such," Owen Watson said.

Someone snickered at the back of the room. Dal jerked his head in that direction, but saw nothing except a few other ranchers wearing a variety of blue jeans, flannel shirts and stoic faces. Each one held a cowboy hat in their lap. Good old boys, with an archaic mentality to match.

"I'm sure you'd hobble, too, if you lost one of your legs. But I guarantee there is nothing wrong with their minds." Julie's voice sounded curt.

"That trail has been there since before my grandpappy was born. It don't need to be changed now for a bunch of city kids that got no business being up there in the first place," Owen said.

Dal grit his teeth. A barrel-chested man with a full gray beard, Owen had dominated the ranching business around Stokely for more than thirty years. Dal had tried to warn Julie about these biases, but even he hadn't expected this unreasonable argument. Not from a man who went to church every week and claimed he was a Christian.

"You're wrong, Mr. Watson." Julie met Owen's glare with one of her own. "Every one of those kids has a right to be up on that trail, the same as you. And it's my job to enforce the law, even if I have to call in the sheriff to do so."

Bravo! Dal wanted to stand up and cheer. He'd been worried about this meeting, with good reason. After what Lyn Baldwin had contended with back when she'd been the ranger and had to round up the wild mustangs in the area, he knew the small-town mentality was frequently difficult to deal with. But Julie seemed to be holding her own.

A swell of pride filled Dal's chest. When he considered who Julie was and where she'd come from, he couldn't help admiring her courage and professionalism.

Owen made a harrumphing sound deep

in the back of his throat. His heavy jowls bunched out like a bristly porcupine. Dal couldn't believe the lack of charity in the other man. His bias aimed at the amputee kids was cruel and bigoted.

"You watch and see." Owen's loud voice blasted the room. "Those kids will start a forest fire up there, or leave their trash all around the mountains. Right now, things is mighty nice up there when we want to go hunting, and we don't want no changes. I don't want to have to evacuate my place if those kids start a wildfire."

A murmur of agreement filtered through the small crowd, almost devoid of women. Dal sucked back a harsh breath. He gazed at Julie, wondering what she'd say next. She didn't breathe. Didn't move a muscle for a very long time.

"You don't know that, Mr. Watson," she said. "The kids from Sunrise Ranch have constant adult supervision. They aren't going to run around starting wildfires any more than you are. Your accusations are completely unfounded." Her voice sounded clipped and filled with disdain.

Owen jutted his chin toward Dal. "Let's speak plain, Miss Granger. I can see how you have a soft spot for those kids, you being a woman and all."

Julie's eyes narrowed, her spine stiffening like a board. "Yes, let's speak plainly, Mr. Watson. Those children have a right to use Gilway Trail. Your words are offensive. And if you can't speak more civilly, then I'll be forced to call an end to this meeting right now."

What a woman. Dal relaxed back in his seat, confident that Julie could handle this situation. He smiled, thinking she was the most remarkable person in the world.

She looked around the room. Numerous ranchers and a couple of other townsfolk sat on the hard metal chairs, listening intently. And Billie Shining Elk, one of the Toyakoi Shoshone tribal leaders. A man who carried a particular dislike for Cade Baldwin. Dal didn't know all the details, but it had something to do with a past familial dispute that happened long before Cade was even born. But that didn't seem to matter to Billie. He still held a forty-year-old grudge. Sitting two rows over, the Native American had twin streaks of gray marring his otherwise jet-black hair. He wore a denim shirt accented by a turquoise bolo tie, his long hair ornamented by a single white-and-gray feather. Dal knew Billie's presence at this meeting didn't bode well for Julie or Sunrise Ranch.

"Are there any more rude comments? If so, you can keep them to yourselves." Julie looked at each person in turn. She ignored Billie's piercing stare, almost daring him to make a derogatory remark.

Dal bit his tongue. An explosion of words swirled around inside his mind. He'd promised Julie to hear everyone out. To listen to their comments with respect and let her handle this meeting. But Owen had crossed the line ten minutes earlier.

Owen sat back in his chair and wrapped his beefy hands across his middle. Nudging Harley Bennett, the rancher sitting next to him, he mumbled something about city folks and how the whole world was falling to pieces.

"Are there any legitimate questions or concerns about the proposed alterations?" Julie gestured to the front of the room where she'd set up a map of the area, diagrams and large pictures she'd had blown up especially for this meeting.

Owen shot his hand into the air. "I've got one. Ain't it true that you've been working out at Sunrise Ranch?"

Julie gave a sharp nod. "Yes, I work there voluntarily in the evenings."

"That's a conflict of interest, ma'am. You work for the Forest Service, yet you're out there working with them cripples."

An audible gasp swept the room and Dal came out of his seat so fast, he even startled himself.

Julie lifted a hand of caution, and Dal bit his tongue before sitting back down. He locked his jaw, forcing himself to shut up and maintain control. But it wasn't easy. Right now, Dal felt like pounding something. And Owen Watson's face would suit that purpose just fine. But he realized that responding to bigotry with violence wouldn't accomplish anything worthwhile.

"You're obviously biased," Owen said.

Julie shook her head. "I'm not biased in the least. In fact, I would suggest that you're the one who is biased. What I do on my own time is my personal business, Mr. Watson."

"Well, you're obviously a cripple lover."

Her eyes widened, her mouth tight. "Excuse me?"

"You heard me. I didn't stutter." He snorted and waved his hand in the air.

Julie's eyes shot daggers, and she sucked in a deep breath. "Mr. Watson, you have made it clear how you feel about this project. Now, let me be perfectly clear. I've studied this proposal at great length and see no reason not to move forward with the alterations. Your complaints are groundless and based on nothing more than personal prejudice. I'm going to proceed with this project. If you do anything to impede the work,

I'll call in the sheriff so fast it'll make your head spin. Do I make myself clear?"

Owen growled a slur beneath his breath, but loud enough that everyone in the room heard him plain enough. A horrible, crude name that should never be spoken out loud. Julie inhaled a sharp breath of offense.

That did it. Dal stood, his hands fisted by his sides. No one was going to call Julie a name like that and get away with it. Not while he had breath in his body. He leveled his glower on Owen. "Mr. Watson, you'd better apologize to Miss Granger right now."

"Or what?" Owen sneered. "You gonna try and make me, cripple?"

"Yes, I will. I may be a cripple, but I'm still man enough to beat you to a pulp." Dal's gaze narrowed. Anger boiled inside him like scalding water. He'd taken a lot of criticism since the war and endured a barrage of rude comments and stares over the years. His temper rarely got the better of him, but right now, he wasn't about to tolerate anyone calling Julie a filthy name.

"Gentlemen! Really? I don't think we

need to resort to violence, do we?" Julie asked with incredulity.

"We do if Mr. Watson won't apologize," Dal said.

"You'd better apologize, Owen." Harley Bennett waved a warning at the other man. "Dal's a former marine. He knows how to fight. He got the Navy Cross for bravery during battle. You'd better apologize to the ranger, or Dal will pound you into sand."

"And I'm afraid I'll be obliged to help him."

Everyone turned to look at Billie Shining Elk. The Shoshone chief didn't move a muscle, but his dark eyes gleamed like black olives as he gazed steadily at Owen.

"But Billie..." Owen sputtered.

"Dal's given a lot for our country, and that counts for something big in my book," Billie said. "You'd better apologize to the ranger before we have to hurt you real bad."

A flash of doubt filled Owen's eyes. Bullies usually counted on their cronies to support their abuse. But now Owen's friends were abandoning him.

Owen looked away, looked at the door, looked anywhere but at Dal and Julie. And that was when Dal realized there was no bite in Owen's bark. Just a mean, cankered soul.

With all the bad blood between Cade and Billie, Cade was not going to believe this situation when Dal told him about it later tonight. Billie had made it clear in the past that he didn't like Cade, or Dal for that matter, but Billie respected their military service. And that meant a lot.

"So what's it gonna be?" Dal asked. "Are you gonna apologize to the lady, or are we gonna take this outside?"

"I, um..."

"Owen Arliss Watson! What in heaven's name do you think you're doing?"

In unison, they all turned and looked at the door as a hefty woman with short, spiky blond hair lumbered up the aisle.

Ah, good. Dal hid a little smile, knowing what was coming. Darlene Watson had arrived, and Dal knew she'd take care of Owen quick enough. All it took was a good woman to make a big, abusive man behave.

* * *

Julie didn't know what to think. She stood her ground, wondering if everyone in the room had gone crazy. Including her and Dal. She could just imagine the forest supervisor's expression when he found out this simple meeting had ended in a brawl out on the street. Somehow, she had to get this crowd under control. Surely someone could talk sense into Owen Watson. But she had no idea what to do about Dal.

She stared at the large woman who'd entered the building like a blast from a grenade. Julie didn't recognize her, but that wasn't odd since she was still fairly new in town.

"Uh-oh. There's Darlene," someone whispered.

What did that mean? Who was Darlene? And why was everyone so afraid of her?

Owen gave an audible groan and dropped his chin to his chest. Darlene shambled past the rows of empty chairs and stopped midway in the room, placing her hands on her ample hips. She glared a hole through the center of Owen's head. His face flushed as red as a watermelon on the Fourth of July and looked ready to explode.

"Didn't I tell you not to come here tonight?" Darlene scolded. "When I got home and found you gone, I knew just where you'd gone. How can you have so little charity toward these children? They're just little, innocent kids. They deserve a nice place to play and have fun for a while."

Ah! Recognition filled Julie's brain. Darlene must be Owen's wife.

"Why, um, I just thought…" Owen blustered.

"You get out that door right now. We're going home. And you're not gonna say one more word about the development of Gilway Trail. You'll leave these good folks alone. They're doing something good for our community." She stepped to the side and tapped her foot on the worn carpet, waiting for Owen to precede her out the door.

Owen hesitated for several seconds, glancing at Harley and Billie for help. But it was false bravado. Harley looked away, offering no support. Billie just looked through the man as if he wasn't even there.

"And you just wait until you get home, Harley Bennett." Darlene waggled a thick finger at the other man. "Your wife's looking for you, too."

Harley's mouth dropped, his eyes flying wide-open.

"Uh-huh. I see you understand real well," Darlene said.

Owen stood and stared straight ahead as he walked toward the door. Taking his cue, Harley stumbled to his feet and followed at a quick trot.

"Just a minute, Mr. Watson," Dal called to Owen's retreating back. "You still owe Miss Granger an apology. Right now."

Julie didn't move. Didn't breathe. She knew the next few moments would resolve this problem for good or bad.

Owen came to a dead halt, coughed and tugged at the buttoned collar of his flannel shirt. Glancing over his burly shoulder at Julie, he spoke very low and very fast. "I'm sorry, ma'am."

With that, he scurried out the door. Darlene inclined her head toward Julie. "Sorry to have bothered you tonight, Ranger. I would have been here earlier, but I had to pick my daughter up from cheerleading practice. You won't have any more trouble from my husband, I can promise you that."

Julie smiled her appreciation, grateful that Darlene had shown up when she did. The meeting had turned ugly, something she hadn't expected, in spite of Dal's warnings. But now the trouble appeared to be over.

Darlene turned and followed her husband and Harley outside, closing the door behind her with a hollow thud.

The room seemed to release a sigh of relief. As though a tornado had passed through, but the danger was now gone.

Julie faced the rest of the group, who seemed overly quiet all of a sudden. "Are there any more questions about this project?"

She hoped no one raised their hands. She waited, counting to three silently in her head. No one moved. No one so much as fluttered an eyelash.

"Good. We'll end our meeting, then. Good night."

Turning, she erased the board with vigorous swipes, then gathered up the maps and pictures. She tried to act normal, but her hands were trembling, her breathing shallow. She ignored it and kept moving. Eager to get out of here as fast as she could. She wanted to go home and bolt the door. To put this horrible meeting behind her.

The room quieted after a few minutes, and she thought she was alone. Swiveling around, she reached for her purse and froze. Dal still sat in his seat, watching her with a mix of admiration and disbelief.

"Dal. I didn't know you were still here."

Putting aside her purse, she walked over to him. Sitting in a chair on the row in front of him, she turned her body so she could look at him face-to-face.

He shrugged. "It's dark outside, so I wanted to wait around and walk you to your car. Just to make sure you're safe."

His consideration touched her heart. Especially since she was still rattled by what had occurred. She'd been railed at and called a despicable name by an angry rancher. Everything short of being threatened with bodily harm. Going outside alone in the dark after such a volatile meeting held no appeal for her. She still couldn't believe how Dal had defended her. "Would you have really taken Mr. Watson outside and beat him up?"

Dal nodded. "Yes, if he hadn't apologized to you. But I would have let him take the first swing. If I've learned one thing in my life, it's that once you draw the line, you've got to be prepared to back it up. And I wasn't about to let him get away with offending you like that. No self-respecting man would allow that."

She rested a forearm against the back of her chair and considered his words. "You remember in tenth grade how you punched Greg Moulton in the nose after you found out he'd been spying on me in the girls' locker room?"

He lifted one brow, and his lips twitched. "Yeah, but that wasn't an even match. The weasel only weighed ninety-five pounds soaking wet. I wanted to teach him a lesson without hurting him too badly."

She laughed, knowing Dal could have pummeled the other boy to bits. Then they both grew quiet, each of them lost within their own memories. She figured it wasn't very Christian to threaten to beat someone up, but she liked that Dal had stood up for her.

"Even back then, you always defended me," she said. "You tried so hard to protect me after Mom and Dad were killed. I…I don't think I ever thanked you for that, Dal. You were there for me, during those dark days following their funeral. I felt so lost, but you kept telling me everything would be okay. And though it hasn't been easy, you were right. I survived."

He waved a dismissive hand and gave her a tight smile. "Ah, you never needed anybody. You were always so spunky. So good at everything you did."

She looked down, twisting her fingers in her lap. She released a shaky breath. "No matter how strong we are, I think we all need someone, Dal. I've been on my own for so long. And I'd forgotten how good it feels to have someone on my side. It means a lot that you stood up for me."

He didn't respond for several long, pounding moments.

"I was proud of you tonight. You really are good at your job," he said.

"Thank you. So are you. The work you do with the kids at Sunrise Ranch is remarkable. And we're going to proceed with our plans for Gilway Trail. The vicious comments voiced at this meeting won't stop our work. I just want you to know that."

"Good. Thank you."

A swelling silence followed. So much for praise and gratitude. Even sitting next to him, Julie still felt miles away from this man she couldn't stop thinking about.

She stood. "Well, it's late. I ought to get home."

"Let me walk you out." He joined her,

grasping the handles of the two heavy bags she'd filled with pictures and maps.

Together, they stepped outside into the moonlight. The swish of the sprinkler system filled the evening air, along with a light dusting of water.

At her car, Dal made sure she was inside, the doors securely locked. While he watched, she started the engine and lowered her window. "Good night, Dal."

"Good night." He tipped the brim of his imaginary hat and stepped away.

As she put the car into gear and pulled out of the parking lot, she looked in her rearview mirror. He stood where she'd left him, his hands in his pants pockets. Tall and lean. And more handsome than a man had a right to be. He didn't move as she switched on her blinker and looked both ways before turning onto the dark, abandoned road.

As he disappeared from view, Julie felt suddenly empty inside. And during the short drive home, all she could think about was how much she missed him.

Chapter Thirteen

"Come on, Marcus! It's your turn."

Standing on a wooden elevated platform set up on the incline of McClellan Mountain, Julie reached for the zip line chair. Down below at the braking platform, children waved their arms in encouragement. Their laughter and squeals of excitement punctuated the air as they recounted their swift journey over the treetops below. Two kids stood beside Julie, awaiting their turn on the thirty-mile-per-hour ride—Marcus and a six-year-old girl named Penny.

"Why don't you go first? I can wait." Marcus stepped back and nudged Penny forward.

"You sure?" The girl smiled wide, showing a missing tooth in front.

"Of course. I've done it zillions of times. I want you to have fun this time."

Julie stared at Marcus, hardly able to believe the dramatic change in him. This was a new turn of events. Marcus's polite behavior to the other children was becoming the new normal. Since that night in Polly's stall several weeks earlier, when he'd sobbed his grief on Julie's shoulder, Marcus had changed. Instead of demanding constant attention, he'd started helping out at Sunrise Ranch. Doing chores with Kristen. Peeling potatoes in the kitchen with a special hand prosthesis Cade had designed. Fetching things for the other amputee kids. Encouraging them not to be nervous as they went horseback riding and flew down the zip line for the first time. Fun and outgoing. Supportive and caring. In fact, Marcus had fast become the most popular child at Sunrise Ranch.

What had made the difference? Julie wasn't sure, but she figured it was because he now felt wanted and needed. Two things every person craved. But she still worried about what might happen to him when he left the ranch at summer's end.

Over the top of Marcus's head, Julie's gaze locked with Dal's. He gave her a knowing smile, then shrugged as if to say, "I don't know, either."

"I—I'm kinda scared," Penny confessed.

The girl's blue helmet drooped over her brows, and she pushed it back on her head. Marcus leaned over and brushed one of her long braids to the side before struggling to tighten the chin strap. He couldn't do it with one hand, and Julie interceded. Rather than snapping at her, he accepted her help without comment. Standing back, he waited patiently for her to finish the task. Then he took Penny's hand in his and led her over to the chair.

"There's no need to be afraid. I'll be right behind you," he told the little girl. He handed her a kid-size pair of leather gloves and helped her tug them on. "See, you'll be strapped into this chair. The harness is strong." He pointed at the heavy cable overhead. "The wire's very strong, too. It can hold up to five thousand pounds."

"Wow! Five thousand pounds?" Penny said the words with awe.

"Yep, so you'll be fine."

Dal helped Marcus get Penny in the chair. After the boy had snapped all the carabiner clips into place, Dal checked to make sure they were secure.

"When did you do this last?" Penny asked Marcus, her voice wobbly with uncertainty.

"Just yesterday. You're gonna fly like a bird. You'll love it."

The girl clasped her hands together in her lap. Her prosthetic leg swung free over the wooden ramp.

"Don't forget your safety goggles." Marcus handed them over and watched as Penny put them on.

Dal tightened the strap around her head, working as a team with Marcus. A perfect pair.

Julie stood back, watching in silence. Normally, Dal was the one offering the kids encouragement on their first zip line ride. But Marcus had assumed that chore. It was Tuesday, and she wondered why she'd taken the afternoon off to come here to work today. She wasn't really needed, yet Cade had invited her. She'd wanted to go on the zip line herself. In all honesty, she couldn't blame Penny for being nervous.

"Okay, now remember what I said. Just hold on to the handlebar and have fun." Marcus placed her hands on the long bar hanging just over her head. She gripped it like a lifeline, her eyes wide and uncertain.

"Ready?" Dal asked.

The girl took a big gulp of air, her lips tightening with determination. She stared straight ahead at the other kids waiting down below the mountain. Finally, she nodded.

Dal released the lever and Penny shot away like a hawk. Faster and faster, she flew over the canopy of treetops below. The other kids at the braking platform went wild, yelling, screaming encouragement, whooping with joy.

Above all the racket, Penny's shrill scream could be heard as she zipped down the hill. Within moments, the trolley connecting the chair hit the block attached to the cable. The twenty-foot bungee cord anchored to an enormous fir tree slowed the chair, and Penny came to a gentle, rocking stop.

Marcus hopped up and down, waving his arms in the air. "Yeah! She did it. Did you see that?"

He grinned at Dal.

"Yep, I saw." Dal's deep laughter rumbled in his chest as the little boy hugged his waist.

Once again, Julie couldn't believe the difference in Marcus. He was acting like a normal, happy child. And she couldn't help feeling partly responsible.

"That was very nice of you, letting Penny go first." She wrapped her arms around Marcus from behind and gave him a quick squeeze. He didn't resist. She brushed a jagged thatch of bangs out of his eyes. The boy didn't say anything, but she could tell by the way he hugged her back that he felt content.

A feeling of exhilaration swept her from head to toe. The joy of service to someone else. How she loved her experiences here at Sunrise Ranch. How she loved this little boy who had no parents to care for him.

Working with these kids made Julie feel invincible and happy. As though she was getting to experience all these activities for the first time, just like the children. And deep inside, she wished she could be their mom.

Finally, she released Marcus and he picked up his own goggles and helmet.

"Okay, Marcus. Your turn." Dal attached the next chair to the cable.

As Julie helped strap the boy in, she almost butted heads with Dal. He bumped her cheek with his nose and she drew away sharply. The close contact with him made her face heat up like road flares.

Dal didn't seem to notice.

"You all ready?" Dal asked Marcus.

The boy nodded, looking first at Dal, then at Julie. His entire face glowed with contentment. "I sure love you guys. You know, I wish you were my new parents. I wish I could stay here at Sunrise Ranch forever."

Julie's breath hitched in her chest. "Why, Marcus, that's the nicest thing anyone's ever said to me."

Dal stood back, a stiff smile curving his lips. "Have fun."

He released the lever, speeding Marcus on his way.

Leaving Julie on the platform alone with Dal.

"He's an amazing boy," she said after Marcus was gone.

"Yeah, he sure is."

"Can you believe he said those things to us?"

Dal didn't respond. She waited for him to comment on Marcus's confession of love, but he didn't say another word. Looking at Dal's tight profile, she thought he was the most wonderful man in the world. Marcus loved him, and so did she. And in that moment, a thought occurred to her. A crazy idea that might lead to nothing. And yet, she felt the overwhelming conviction that she must try.

"Dal, Marcus didn't mean anything by what he said."

He looked down at his booted feet. "Oh, I think he meant every word."

"And is that so bad? Being a family with me, I mean?"

He gave her a fleeting look. "No, of course not."

"Then you liked Marcus's idea?"

A fierce red color flooded his cheeks. "I…I didn't pay it much heed. He's a little boy who's incredibly lonely."

So was Dal. So was Julie. But it was obvious that Dal didn't want to pursue this topic, so she let it drop. Deep inside, she realized that something had changed for her. Something at the core of her soul. She didn't know how or why, but she no longer liked being alone. And she decided to do something about it.

"You're next." Dal reached for another chair, his movements rigid and unapproachable.

"Dal, are you okay?"

"Sure." He nodded, not looking at her. Shutting her out.

"I hadn't planned to ride the zip line." She stepped back, her long ponytail bouncing. "Is it chicken of me to admit that I'm a bit nervous, too?"

That brought a half smile to his handsome face. "No, of course not. But you need to do it at least once. To show the kids that you're not afraid."

But that was just it. She *was* afraid. Not only of the two-hundred-foot cable and the twenty-foot drop, but of what Dal and Sunrise Ranch had come to mean to her. Still, she wanted this more than anything else.

She wanted Dal.

"Come on," he encouraged. "The ride will be over in just a few minutes."

He reached for her, his calloused palm warm and gruff against the skin of her arm.

"Is it as easy as it looks?" She sat in the chair while he buckled her in tight.

"Easier." But he didn't smile as he secured the clips. In fact, he seemed so reserved now. As if he didn't want to be near her anymore.

"You're not just trying to get rid of me, are you?" she asked in a teasing voice.

He jerked his head up, looking surprised. "No, of course not."

But then he turned away, his back to her. Standing aside while she tugged her leather gloves over her hands.

Something was wrong. No doubt Marcus's words had upset him, but she didn't know why. It was just wishful thinking of a sweet little boy having fun. It didn't mean anything. Not really. But Julie found herself wishing that…

"Ready?" Dal asked.

She gave two quick nods. Her heart beat madly inside her chest. Her breathing sped up, and she gripped the handlebar tight.

Dal released the lever and she zipped forward like a racehorse out of the starting gate. The chair picked up speed, the wind rushing past her face. A scream of pure pleasure rose upward in her chest. The trees below looked small and insignificant, yet she knew they were huge. She felt free and powerful. Filled with vitality and life.

Filled with joy.

As she approached the braking platform, the trolley smacked the brake block and she jolted ever so slightly. Her legs swung high off the ground as she came to a nice and easy stop. Tucking her knees in, she waited for Cade to pull her over to the platform with the bungee cord. The kids cheered, bouncing up and down. After Cade helped her out of the harness, children swarmed all around her. Again, Marcus was right there, his little arms wrapped around her in a hearty hug. Generous words of accomplishment filled the air as the children congratulated one another. This had been an incredible experience Julie wanted to share with Dal.

Whirling around, she shaded her eyes against the bright sunlight and looked up the hill. Dal stood on the launch, just watching her. A forlorn figure. All alone.

She lifted her arm and gave a big wave, but he turned away. Hadn't he seen her? What was bothering him? He just wasn't acting like his usual outgoing self. Not since Marcus had said he loved them and wished they were his parents. Surely that hadn't upset Dal so much.

Or had it?

Several staff members directed the kids down the trail toward the ranch. They were planning to ride the horses next. Dal would introduce them to Polly, something Julie never got tired of. Julie soon found herself alone with Cade.

"What's Dal doing?" she asked. "Isn't he going to ride the zip line down the mountain?"

She pointed to where Dal was coming down the steps to the platform and taking the long way down the hill.

"Apparently not." Cade gathered up the equipment, and she paused beside him.

In spite of his prosthetic leg, Dal had chosen to walk the thin path that wound through the thick trees. He obviously wanted to be by himself for a time.

"He's so lonely," she said. "I can't get him to open up. It's as though he's keeping something from me."

Cade picked up a bungee cord and began wrapping it around his arm in a tidy coil. His gaze followed Dal as he disappeared behind the trees. "Yeah, I know."

"You know? What do you know?"

Cade pursed his lips. "You need to talk to Dal. It's not my place to disclose his secrets, Julie."

"He has a secret? Something else I don't know?"

Cade heaved a heavy sigh. "Yes, but I shouldn't have said even that much. It's for Dal to talk about when he's ready, not me."

So. Dal was keeping something from her. Something that obviously rested heavy on his mind. But what could it be? She couldn't fault Cade for not telling her. Good friends didn't do that, and Cade was a good friend to Dal.

"I just wish I knew how to help him," she said.

"You care about him."

She glanced at him, her cheeks flooding with warmth. "Does it show?"

He nodded. "I'm afraid so. You light up like a sunbeam every time he's near."

Her gaze scanned the tree line, looking for Dal to emerge along the walk path. "I've tried not to care, but can't seem to help myself. It's been that way since we were in high school. Something about Dal connects with my spirit."

"Do you love him?" he asked.

Yes! But thinking that and saying it out loud were two different things. Weren't they?

"I…I think I need to take this slow." It was a clumsy way to evade his question, but she wasn't yet ready to admit the obvious. At least not until she knew how Dal felt about her.

Cade placed a comforting hand on her shoulder. "He loves you, too. He just refuses to admit it. I think both of you have been badly hurt and will have to come to terms with your pasts if either of you ever want to have a future together. Dal's gonna have to help himself, Julie. Just don't give up on him. He's got to work this out in his own mind first. But maybe Lyn and I can help speed up the process."

She quirked a brow at him. "What do you mean?"

He stepped past her and picked up the toolbox. "Oh, nothing. Don't worry about it right now."

He stepped down off the platform and headed toward the path leading back to the ranch. Julie watched him go, her thoughts a riot of unease. What did he mean? What was he planning to do? And why was it such a covert affair?

Oh, she didn't like this situation. No, not at all. She had strong feelings for Dal. She could no longer deny it. She'd pushed him away many years ago. Out of embarrassment and to protect him from being hurt, too. Now she wanted to be with him all the time. When she was alone, she was always thinking about him. She couldn't get him off her mind. But that would have to change. And soon.

Chapter Fourteen

The moment Dal stepped inside the bowling alley on Saturday night, he knew he shouldn't be there. A fun night out, Cade had said. With just him and Lyn. Kristen was old enough to babysit Marcus and Clarisse for a few hours. The adults would eat pizza, bowl a few games and have a few laughs. An evening free from work and responsibilities. What could it hurt?

As he retrieved his bowling shoes and stepped past the main counter, Dal looked across the expanse of bowling lanes. The crash of pins being knocked down filled the air, along with happy chatter from patrons and the acrid scent of spicy hot wings.

Cade sat at the square desk of a bowling lane, no doubt setting up their scoring sheet. Seeing his friend, Dal took a step in that direction. Julie's name flashed across the overhead screen. Dal froze. The bottoms of his shoes seemed stuck to the floor. He couldn't move. Couldn't take a deep breath.

He scanned the bowling alley, his gaze screeching to a halt when he saw Julie. She stood beside Lyn in front of a rack of bowling balls. The two women laughed together as they hefted several of the balls, testing the weight and comfort in their hands.

Julie looked up and met his gaze. Her mouth dropped open and her eyes widened. Her hand swung downward to her side, the ten-pound bowling ball hanging loose from three of her fingers. And then Dal knew. Cade had set them both up. Julie hadn't known Dal would be here, either. But now that they'd seen each other, it would be awkward to try to escape gracefully.

"Hi, Dal!" Lyn called with a smile.

Hearing his wife's greeting, Cade turned, caught sight of Dal and waved an arm. "Hi, buddy. Come on over. I've got the scorecard all set up and ready to go. The pizza will be here momentarily."

Dal fumed silently. He was half tempted to ignore his meddling friends and turn and walk straight out the door. But this wasn't Julie's fault. And no matter how much Dal sought to avoid her, he couldn't bring himself to hurt her intentionally.

Tossing an angry glare at Cade, Dal crossed to their lane and stepped down into the seating area. Whether he liked it or not, he would have to sit through an evening of bowling and eating pizza with his two best friends and the woman of his dreams. Not so unpleasant, under normal circumstances. But Dal figured it would be pure torture. Being near Julie. Laughing and having fun. And not being able to tell her how he really felt about her. He silently prayed he could make it through the evening.

Such a strange turn of events. When he'd first met Julie again that day she'd sprained her ankle, he'd had a zillion questions for her, had been eager to renew their friendship. But now he wanted to stay away. Because he loved her. Because he had nothing to offer her. Just a broken and scarred body. Pursuing Julie now would only bring both of them more pain.

"Hi, Dal," Julie greeted him with a tentative smile.

Dal hated the hesitant look in her eyes, knowing she must sense his reticence. "Hi, Jules."

Her smile widened, and he thought she kind of liked him to call her by that name. It seemed too familiar. The name had slipped out, a memory of when they'd been two naive, innocent kids.

"I figured we could play teams." Cade completely ignored the withering stare Dal turned on him. "Dal and Julie will play against Lyn and me."

Julie took a slow inhale and tilted her head toward Dal in a shy glance. "I hope you don't regret having me as your partner. I haven't bowled in years, and I doubt I'm very good."

He regretted it already. Not because of

her, but because of what she made him feel. And yet, because he loved her, he couldn't bring himself to do anything but encourage her. "Don't worry. You'll do just fine."

Going to the racks, he quickly chose a worn, sixteen-pound urethane ball and set it in the return area of their lane. On his way back to the seats, he leaned over Cade's shoulder and whispered for his ears alone. "Don't think you're off the hook, pal. You and me are gonna have a long chat later tonight, once we're alone."

Throwing back his head, Cade laughed. "Oh, I can't wait."

Dal tossed him a hefty glower that didn't seem to dent Cade's enthusiasm in the least. Dal noticed the two women's quizzical expressions and looked away. Julie didn't say anything and Lyn quickly changed the subject. No doubt she was in on Cade's scheme to get him and Julie together.

"Why don't we take a few practice frames? You want to go first, Julie?" Lyn sat on the hard-backed bench and crossed her legs.

"Okay." Julie stood and held her right hand

over the air vent to dry any moisture off her fingers. Dressed in knee-length capris, she wore a lavender shirt with short sleeves. White socks hugged her trim ankles, her feet encased in a pair of drab brown-striped shoes issued by the bowling alley. Instead of her normal ponytail, she wore her long hair loose around her shoulders. Feminine and pretty.

And Dal couldn't take his eyes off her.

He blinked as she carefully pressed her fingers into the holes and picked up her ball. With the tip of her tongue pressed against her upper lip, she stepped over to the approach, supporting the heavy ball with both hands. She paused as she sighted down the lane, then ran a bit toward the foul line, drew back her arm and let the ball fly. Dal caught himself staring at her slender legs and looked away. The ball thudded onto the lane and promptly rolled into the gutter.

Julie groaned and whirled around, her face a contortion of disgust. Her eyes met his in a repentant smile. "Don't say I didn't warn you."

"Don't worry," he encouraged. "You're just warming up."

When her ball returned, she tried again, with the same results. A gutter ball.

Without a word, she returned to the seats and plopped down beside him. He caught the delicate fragrance of her shampoo and tried not to inhale too deeply.

No one spoke as Lyn took her practice turn. On her first roll, she knocked down eight pins, but missed the last two on her second throw.

"Good try!" Cade gave a loud whoop. As he stood to take his turn, he hugged his wife tight, whispering something in her ear. She giggled and swatted his shoulder.

And Dal wished he dared act that way with Julie. Like a real couple. Like they were in love and had the world in the palm of their hands.

Dal went last, frustrated enough to throw a strong, spinning ball that battered down all the pins in one strike.

Julie clapped and cheered for him. In spite of his anger at Cade, Dal couldn't help being pleased. It'd been a long time since he'd been out on a date with a beautiful woman, and his fear warred with his desire to be with Julie.

They soon started the game. This time, they would keep score. With concentration creasing her brow, Julie launched her ball toward the pin deck, but it rolled straight into the gutter. She stood there, a frown marring her brow. Dal couldn't stand to see her so dejected.

Walking over to her, he handed her another ball. Then he proceeded to give her some pointers. He stood with his chest close to her back, his arms around her to help support the ball. As he showed her how to draw her arm back straight, tendrils of her clean, lemon-scented hair tickled his chin. She turned her face to the side, listening to his instructions. His lips brushed against her warm cheek. A blast of awareness swept through him. Like a lightning rod, he zoned in on her magnetic attraction.

"Okay, thanks. I think I can do it now," she whispered.

He stepped away and watched while she swung back her arm and let the ball fly down the alley. An explosion of sound filled the air as the ball plowed into the pins, knocking over all but one.

"Yes! I did it. Thank you, Dal." She gave a little hop and fisted her right hand in the air.

Twirling around, she sought his gaze. He caught the eager glint in her eyes, the hope for his approval. He couldn't help returning her wide smile.

"That's what I'm talking about. Well done," he said.

She beamed, her face glowing like an angel's. He felt beyond proud of her accomplishment. Above all else, he wanted this woman to succeed. To be happy. It wouldn't do himself or her any good to scowl and act grumpy just because Cade had set them up on a blind date without their knowledge.

On her next go-around, Julie stood poised with her right hand over the air vent, waiting for the conveyer to do its work. When her ball appeared, she picked it up and stepped over to the line. She ran up to the line in a way that was distinctly her own style, and Dal gawked at the gentle swing of her hips. Again, he looked away, but not for long. At the thud of the ball, he stood and watched with rapt attention as it swept down the shiny planks of hard maple and struck the last pin.

"Yay!" She hopped up and down.

"That's my girl," he called, delighted by her efforts.

Then he realized what he'd said and clamped his mouth shut. He must remain alert and be careful with his words. He must maintain control. For both of their good.

"I'm afraid we might be in trouble. These two are pretty good." Lyn smiled at her husband.

"Julie's a fast learner. The pressure is on." Cade glanced at Dal. "Your turn, buddy."

"I'm not your buddy tonight. This is war," Dal growled as he retrieved his bowling ball and moved over to the approach. With a powerful swing, he stepped forward and launched the ball down the lane.

"Strike!" he called as the pins exploded

into a pile. The sweep mechanism pushed the pins backward off the lane.

Turning, he walked to the seating area while Cade logged his score.

"Yep, you're definitely in trouble tonight." Dal gave his friend a potent look. If he got no other revenge, he planned to beat Cade tonight.

Cade merely smiled good-naturedly and winked at Lyn. "Your turn, hon."

They all laughed and thoroughly enjoyed themselves. Dal couldn't stay upset at Cade for long. They were too close and had a long history together. Since Dal was already here, he might as well have fun. In a way, he felt like a Cinderella man. This evening couldn't last, and when it ended, he'd turn back into a plain old cripple and return to his regular lonely life.

On Dal's third frame, he got another strike—three in a row.

"Turkey!" Julie called buoyantly.

He spun around and spiked one of his brows upward. "Are you calling me a turkey?"

"No, but when you get three strikes in a row, it's called a turkey. Isn't it?"

He laughed. "So it is."

A short time later, after Dal and Julie had won the first game, they chowed down on an all-meat and cheese pizza. Sitting together in a booth, they laughed as they discussed the funny antics of some of the kids at Sunrise Ranch.

"I can't believe the change in Marcus." Cade spoke to Dal and Julie. "You two sure have made a difference for him."

"Yes, that boy is definitely not the same as he used to be," Lyn agreed. "He's so pleasant and helpful around the ranch lately. His social worker came out to check on him yesterday and said she could hardly believe he was the same child."

Dal jutted his chin toward Julie. "It was Julie's doing, not mine."

Julie's face flushed an attractive shade of pink. "I think we all made a difference for Marcus. It wasn't just one person's doing. It takes a village, you know?"

"Yes, it sure does. But you're amazing with the kids, Julie." Lyn smiled with admiration.

"Thanks," Julie said.

Cade lifted an arm to wrap around Lyn's shoulders. "So when are we gonna start work on Gilway Trail?"

"The fifth of September," Julie said.

Dal rested an elbow on the tabletop. "That's kind of late in the year, isn't it?"

She glanced at him, then looked down at her soft drink. "Not really. It's late enough that the harsh summer heat will be gone, but not so late that we'll be dealing with inclement weather. And that's when the Back Country Horsemen can participate. But don't worry. All of the permits are in order, and we should have the trail and campsite finished by the first of October. You should be able to use the trail next summer without any problems."

"That's great," Cade said. "You've been a big help to us on that project."

"You're welcome," she said.

"Your 5K race is coming up soon, isn't it?" Lyn asked.

Julie nodded. "Yes, in a couple more weeks."

"Are you two gonna be ready?" Cade asked, looking between her and Dal.

"I am, but I don't know about this guy." Julie gave a competitive smile and jerked her thumb toward Dal, who sat beside her in the booth.

"For me, it's just fun. It's not about the competition," Dal said.

"Are you two still running together every morning?" Lyn asked.

Julie took a quick sip of soda from her straw, leaving Dal to answer.

"Um, not lately." Not liking where this subject might lead, he turned his body out of the booth and placed his feet together before standing. "Well, I'm ready for our next match. Let's get to it."

Cade chuckled and stood, taking hold of Lyn's hand to help her up. "You think we can beat them this time?"

"Oh, yeah." She gave him an easy smile.

By the end of the night, the couples were tied.

"Well, that's it for me. I need to get home," Julie said after the final match.

Standing close beside her, Cade looked at Dal. "Can you drive Julie home? We picked her up, but we really need to get home to the kids now."

Dal's jaw dropped. Just when he'd thought Cade could not stoop any lower, he was proved wrong.

Julie didn't say much as Dal drove her home. From the tension in his shoulders, she knew he wasn't happy about it. And she couldn't blame him. Cade and Lyn both meant well, but they were pushing too hard. As much as Julie wished things could be different between them, she realized that Dal wasn't ready to renew their romance. In fact, he might never be ready. And that brought a pang of sorrow to her heart.

He turned on the headlights, then gripped

the steering wheel with both hands as he drove down the dark streets. Not a lot of traffic. Just the calming lights gleaming from the tidy homes in Julie's neighborhood.

Dal pulled into her driveway and killed the engine. Before he could get out of the truck and walk her to her doorstep, she reached out and laid her hand on his arm.

"Dal, I'm sorry about tonight. I know we were both kind of bushwhacked. I hope you're not too upset with Cade."

He pursed his lips together and gave a noncommittal grunt. She couldn't leave it at that. Her mind raced with words she longed to say. With feelings she yearned to express.

"I don't know how you feel about tonight, but this is the best nondate I've ever had." She gave him a heartening smile, hoping to help lighten his mood.

He shifted his hands off the steering wheel, and her fingers slipped away. "Yeah. Lots of fun."

She blinked. His voice sounded mocking. This was a new twist for Julie. Pursuing a man was alien to her. Something she'd avoided all her life. Taking a deep, settling breath, she plunged onward. "Actually, I've been wanting to talk with you for several days now, but we never seem to find time alone anymore."

"Talk about what?" He hitched a shoulder as he stared out the windshield. Not looking at her. Not moving. Just waiting.

"Cade told me that something's bothering you. A big secret you're keeping to yourself."

He turned his head toward her, his eyes narrowed. "Cade had no right to tell you that."

"Don't worry, he didn't confide what it is. And it was my fault. I guessed long ago that something must be bothering you, so I asked him about it."

"And?"

"And he told me to talk to you about it. So what's your secret?"

He snorted. "If I told you, then it wouldn't be a secret anymore."

"You can trust me, Dal. There was a time

when we didn't keep anything from each other."

"Those days are long gone." A cynical undertone tinged his words.

"I'm worried about you. You can tell me about it. You know that."

"No, I can't." His features hardened, his body language telling her that he was anxious to get away. Like a cornered animal, desperate to flee.

Okay, this wasn't going to be as easy as she'd hoped. "Dal, for the longest time I've been alone. All by myself. And it wasn't until I moved to Stokely and met up with you again that I realized I don't like that. I…I want us to be close again. To be dear friends, like we were when we were kids. To trust each other. You see, I've fallen in love with you all over again, and I… I'd like us to take it further."

Okay, she'd laid everything on the table. Her heart and soul, just lying there, waiting for the cleaver to drop.

He spun around and looked at her, his eyes filled with incredulity. "You love me?"

"Yes, Dal. I love you. More than anything else in the world. And…and I'm hoping maybe you can love me again, too."

"Don't say that."

She blinked. "Why?"

"No, this isn't happening. Not now, Julie. Not ever."

"Why? How long are you going to punish me for ending our relationship when we were teenagers? We were just kids, Dal. And I didn't have a lot of choice back then."

"This isn't about that, Julie."

She didn't believe him. He'd never forgiven her for abandoning him. Maybe he never would. "Then what is this about?"

"It has nothing to do with you. I…I don't know what I can ever be with you."

She tilted her head to one side. "You don't have to be anything with me. Just be the Dal I love and it will all work out fine."

He leaned his head back against the seat and clenched his eyes closed. "Oh, Julie. I wish it were that simple. I really do. But you don't understand."

"I'm trying to understand. Really, I am."

He rolled his head in frustration.

"Can't you explain it to me, please?" she asked.

She held perfectly still. Barely daring to hope for a second chance at happiness with the love of her life. Her heart slammed against her ribs. She wanted so much to touch him. To wrap her arms around him and tell him everything would be okay.

"My secret is a dark one," he said.

"So is mine. But that's old history. Can't we leave it there and move on?" Her voice sounded choked. If he could find the courage to tell her about his past, then somehow she could do the same. Because she knew they could have no future together without disclosing everything and taking a leap of faith. A leap of trust.

In each other and the Lord.

He met her gaze, his eyes filled with deep, abiding anguish. When he spoke, his voice sounded strangled by grief. "Okay, you want to know the truth? Then here it is. I may not be able to father a child, Julie. The explosion that took my leg banged me up pretty bad. I was lucky I only lost my leg. I can deal with that. But the damage was worse. The doctors don't know how bad it might be. I was engaged to be married. When my fiancée found out the truth, she dumped me. I… I'm just half a man, Julie. That's all I'll ever be. I'm not husband material. I can never marry you, and that's it."

Her heart twisted in a vise of pain. "Oh, Dal. Don't say that."

"It's the truth. You wanted to know. So now you know." His voice was an angry growl. He'd never spoken to her like this. So annoyed and angry. As though she were an irritating little girl who wouldn't leave him alone.

She tensed, wanting to feel insulted. Wanting to lash out at him in return. But then she thought about the burden he'd carried since he'd returned home from the war. The pain of losing his leg was bad enough. But to lose his fiancée and believe he might never be a father must have crushed him.

"I'm so sorry. So very sorry for all you've lost," she said.

Scooting across the seat, she hugged him, resting her head against his chest. He didn't respond, but she wouldn't let go. Not now. Not ever.

And in an aching whisper, she told him about her past. Everything. About her foster dad, her embarrassment, self-loathing and loss of trust.

"So you see? Each of us has been deeply hurt. And yet, I can't help believing that God can heal our wounds. We've got to let it go, Dal. Because I'm not leaving you ever again. Because I want to be with you for the rest of forever."

She felt the steady rhythm of his heartbeat against her cheek. She breathed in his spicy scent of aftershave and fabric softener. And in those quiet moments, the eyes of her understanding were opened. She knew deep in her heart that God had never abandoned her. Not once. Even during the dark years following her parents' deaths, the Lord had been there for her. And somehow, once she was ready, God had led her back to Dal. A shimmering ray of sunlight in a dark, cruel world.

"You deserve better." Strong emotion pinched Dal's vocal cords.

"We both deserve to be happy, Dal. And you make me incredibly happy."

She held him tighter. Fiercely. Afraid to let go. Ignoring the tears as they streamed down her cheeks.

Finally, after all these years, she'd said the words out loud. The words she'd needed to say in order to cleanse her soul. In order to heal. And as Julie confided all her loss and hurt, Dal whispered a few heartening words against her hair.

"Don't cry. You'll be okay," he said.

She felt so close to Dal and the Lord. For the first time in a long time, she no longer felt alone. If only Dal could accept what she was telling him. If only he could believe it, too.

She cuddled closer in his embrace, but he didn't hug her back.

"You know, there are lots of ways for us to have kids," she said. "Up until a few months ago, I thought I'd live my entire life alone. I thought I had accepted that. But being with you is more than I ever dared hope for. If we don't have children, it's not the end of the world, Dal."

His body went rigid against her. After a moment, he pushed her away. She felt the wall he'd erected between them go up like an iron plate.

"You don't mean that, Julie."

"Yes, I do." She met his eyes, not blinking. Unwilling to let him go.

He shook his head and licked his lips. "Maybe you do now, but years from now, you might feel differently. And then it'd be too late. I can't hurt you that way. I won't do it, Julie."

"Do you trust my commitment so little?" she asked.

"No, it's not that. I just don't want to tie you to me when you could have something better."

"Don't you think it's my right to decide that for myself?" A feeling of desperation buzzed through her head. In spite of her admission, he hadn't told her he loved her. He hadn't said the words, or that he wanted to be with her again, either.

"Y-you're just not what I'm looking for, Julie. I don't see our relationship going any further. I'm sorry if I led you to believe you could expect more. But it's just not there for me."

Oh, that hurt. So badly.

A contrived smile curved his lips, but it didn't reach his eyes. "I had a lot of fun with you tonight, Jules. I'll never forget it."

Opening his door, he got out. She stared at him through the windshield as he walked around to her side of the truck. The heat of mortification burned her face. He didn't love her anymore. When she thought about what she'd said to him tonight, the way she'd practically thrown herself at him, she wanted to disappear into thin air.

She blinked, hardly able to believe what he'd said. They'd had a good time, told each other their deepest, most haunting secrets. And now they would go on and act as if nothing had ever happened between them.

He opened her door and stood back. As

she stepped out, the warm summer evening wind embraced her bare arms. The air smelled of honeysuckle and barbecue. A car passed by on the street, its headlights shining into her eyes. She turned her head away as a dawning realization flooded her entire being.

Dal didn't love her anymore. He hadn't said the words. Oh, he cared, of that she had no doubt. But caring for an old high school sweetheart and loving her enough to commit the rest of his life to her were two very different things.

The heat of mortification rose across her face. In a blind daze, she hurried toward her house. She had to get inside and bolt the door behind her. Right now.

He accompanied her to the front porch, not touching her. Not saying another word. His presence a constant reminder of how she'd opened up her heart and he'd stomped on it. Was that how he'd felt all those years ago when she'd stopped writing to him? As if she'd shredded his heart into teeny little pieces with a meat grinder?

She fumbled inside her purse, blinking at the blinding tears, searching for her keys. They jingled as he took them from her fingers and opened the door. Once she stepped inside and flipped on the living room light, she ducked her head so he wouldn't see how he'd hurt her.

"Good night, Julie." He stepped away.

Then he was gone. She stood there watching as he pulled out of her driveway and sped away. Her heart ached, the pain suffocating her. Her soul cried out with despair. No, this couldn't be happening. It couldn't be real. Surely God wouldn't bring her here and help her recognize her love for Dal and then take it all away a second time. But she realized this wasn't God's fault. It was a choice. Dal's choice.

Closing the door, she leaned against it, her legs too weak to hold her up. A hoarse cry rose upward inside her chest. As she slid down to the floor, her purse dropped from her limp fingers and hit the tiled entranceway. Covering her face with her hands, she wept.

Chapter Fifteen

Two weeks later, Julie drove downtown toward the city park. Though it was just after seven in the morning, she'd been up for almost two hours. Since Dal had rejected her after their bowling date, she hadn't been sleeping well. His words seemed to haunt her.

She wasn't what he was looking for. He didn't love her. And she couldn't get over it.

After eating a fuel-healthy breakfast of oatmeal, she'd been warming up. Anxious for the 5K race. Anxious to see Dal again yet dreading it at the same time.

As she navigated her way through the heavy traffic, she pressed on the brake. People milled around the main gazebo where a platform had been set up for announcements. Looking to the side, she saw an open-air tent with a sign overhead that read Registration. No doubt that was where she should go to pick up her number. The race would begin in twenty minutes, and she had just enough time to check in.

Dressed in her jogging clothes, Julie thrust open the car door and stepped out. The buzz of laughter and voices filtered through the air. The crisp scent of fresh-cut grass swept across the warm breeze. She tossed her jacket into the backseat, then locked and closed the door. Depositing her key into a small zipper bag, she stowed her water bottle on a clip at her waist and walked toward the gazebo.

"Hi, Julie!"

She swiveled around and saw Marcus standing next to the podium, balancing Clarisse on his hip.

"Hi, sweetie." Her heart gave a giant leap as she walked over to the boy she'd come to care so much about. He returned her hug, but finally pushed away when she held on to him a bit too long.

"Are you excited about watching the race?" She reached out and rubbed the baby's chubby arm.

"Yeah. You go over there to get your number." The boy pointed to the registration desk.

"Thanks, I was just headed in that direction. You haven't seen Dal by any chance, have you?"

He crinkled his nose against the bright sunlight streaming through the tall elm trees. "Nope, not yet. He didn't drive in with us this morning."

"Ah. Well, I suspect he'll be here soon." She glanced down at the boy's amputated wrist. "Hey, is that your new cosmetic hand?"

He beamed a happy smile and lifted the hand up for her inspection. "Yeah, it came in yesterday. It looks good, huh?"

She studied the hand-drawn fingernails, crinkle lines and tiny hairs. An exact replica of his other hand. "It sure does. Very lifelike. If I didn't know about your amputation, I couldn't even tell it's not a real hand."

She'd known that Cade had ordered a new cosmetic hand for Marcus and that Dal had paid for it. Dal was generous to a fault, and she loved him more than anything else in the world. Which explained her broken heart. She couldn't seem to get over it and told herself for the umpteenth time to let him go.

"I can't wait to see you run. Cade's over there with Kristen, getting us some hot chocolate," the boy said.

Lifting her head, Julie saw the doctor standing before a booth, counting out coins for a cashier. Kristen and Lyn were with him. Together, they picked up the cups of chocolate and headed her way. When Cade spied Julie, she expected his normally exuberant smile. Instead, he cast a doubtful frown her way and urged Kristen to go ahead of him.

"Hi, Julie. Have you warmed up yet?" Lyn asked in a subdued tone. Her eyes looked red, as if she'd been crying. An odd notion, surely. Maybe it was just allergies.

Julie nodded. "Yeah, have you seen Dal? I was hoping to speak with him before the race."

Lyn shook her head, then leaned against her husband and looked away. Sad and overly quiet.

Cade wrapped an arm around his wife, his gaze resting on his two daughters. "Kristen, why don't you and Marcus take Clarisse back to our seats? We'll join you in a few minutes. I want to talk to Julie alone first."

"Okay." Kristen took the baby and headed toward the bleachers a short distance away.

Marcus accepted his cup of hot chocolate. "But I want to stay with Julie."

"Come on, Marcus. Now!" Kristen called over her shoulder, sounding like an older sister.

"Ah," the boy grumbled, but obeyed.

Lyn's gaze trailed after the children, ever vigilant of her brood. Julie couldn't help doing the same, thinking how her life was about to change.

With or without Dal beside her.

"Good luck, Julie." Marcus waved and hurried to keep up.

"Thanks, honey. I'll see you after the race." Then she faced Cade. "Okay, spill it. What's going on?"

He chewed his bottom lip, his reticence palpable. A heavy foreboding settled over Julie like a damp blanket. Something was wrong here. Maybe Dal had confided in Cade about her declaration of love. And maybe the doctor was displeased with her. But that didn't seem right.

"Is Dal okay?" She tried to play it cool, but inside she was trembling.

"No, he's not," Lyn blurted. "You've got to find him, Julie. Bring him back here. This is his home now. Don't let him chase you off. You two belong together. He's just too stubborn to face it."

"Honey," Cade cautioned. "Let me explain to her first."

"Explain what?" Julie didn't understand any of this, but she knew it wasn't good. At this point, she was nervous as a bee flitting around a flower garden.

"He left, Julie. Early this morning," Cade said.

"What?"

Lyn stepped close and pressed her hand against Julie's shoulder. "I'll leave you alone to speak with Cade, but know that my prayers are with you and Dal. I want him home safe."

Julie stood dumbfounded as the woman followed after the kids. Knots of tension tightened at the nape of her neck. Three words pounded her brain. *Dal had left.* He was gone. But where? When?

She already knew why.

"He doesn't want me." She said the words out loud, as if to herself.

Cade shook his head, his eyes filled with sad light. "I don't believe that's true. In fact, I think you're the reason he left."

"But why?"

"Because he loves you. I think he's afraid."

"But if he loves me, why would he run away?" She didn't understand. Not really.

Not after Dal had told her she wasn't what he wanted.

"Think about it, Julie. It's hard living in this small community and seeing you now and then but not being with you," Cade said.

"But that was his choice."

"Not really. I think it's just what he believes is best for you, not what he wants."

Julie shook her head, not understanding this situation at all. So they might not be able to have kids. Many couples struggled with infertility. They could still be happy and fulfilled together. There was so much more to life than babies.

Wasn't there?

She snorted. "Hogwash! I love him, Cade. I'm almost thirty-six years old. I think I'm old enough to know what I want. And right now, I want Dal. We can sort the children issue out later on. But first I want Dal. No ifs, ands or buts about it."

"Then you're gonna have to convince him it's right for you two to be together. But you'll have to hurry."

A sense of panic struck her. Dal had left.

It might be too late. Even if she could find him, she had already tried to convince him that they should be together. But love was a different matter. She couldn't make him love her.

She glanced at her car. "Where did he go?"

"I don't know. He refused to tell me. He had his truck all packed up early this morning and said he'd call to check in later tonight. He headed out on U.S. 50, but he refused to tell me where he's headed."

She understood. The coward. Dal wouldn't reveal his destination because he knew Cade would tell Julie, and she might come after him. And in that moment, something hardened inside her. Something cold and frantic.

Whirling around, she ran toward the parking lot.

"Where are you going?" Cade yelled after her.

"To find Dal."

"But what about the race?"

"Forget it!"

Julie sprinted past the registration desk,

past the other joggers as they headed for the starting line. She wouldn't be there. Not this year. She was in a different race right now. The race of her life. A race for happiness. To find the man she loved and bring him home.

If she could.

At her car, she fumbled with the key. Her fingers shook as she yanked the door open. She gripped the steering wheel, her knuckles white, her mind spinning with tension. Where would Dal have gone? What if she never saw him again? What if she couldn't find him?

What if he had never really loved her?

She pulled out of the parking lot, jerking on her seat belt at the same time. Trying to control her speed so she didn't run over some pedestrians. But inside, her heart was bursting. She had no idea where to go. Dal had a big head start on her. He could be anywhere by now. Long gone.

And she prayed. Begged God to help her find Dal before it was too late. Begged Him to help Dal love her the way she loved him.

As she left town, she headed out on U.S. 50, pressing the accelerator, trying not to go too much over the speed limit. The long black asphalt stretched out before her. A waterfall of panic washed over her. Even if she found Dal, she had no idea what to say to him. She had no idea what it might take to convince him to return with her.

For fifteen miles, she saw nothing but sagebrush and rolling hills. She passed a few cars, but they weren't Dal's. As she sped by an exit, she craned her neck, hunting for a glimpse of his classic vehicle. Nothing. She didn't see Dal.

And then she did. Standing along the side of the road beside his old blue truck. She blinked to make sure it was him, knowing the curve of his back, the width of his shoulders, the tilt of his head like the back of her hand.

Pure relief swept through her just as a tornado sweeps a house off its foundation. She'd found him. It wasn't too late. He was here. She had another chance. One more chance to convince him they should be together.

The hood of his truck was up, a thin stream of gray smoke spewing from the engine. He leaned over to inspect the problem, then raked a hand through his short hair.

She slowed her car, pulling over on the side of the road. He drew back from the truck and glanced back at her. When he recognized her, his face contorted with surprise. A look of frustration marred his handsome features. Then he shook his head, as though it were a shame. As though the end of the world had finally come.

Well, tough. He wasn't getting away from her again. No, not until she'd had her say. She just had to make him understand. And she prayed harder than ever before that God would make Dal believe her words.

Of all the rotten luck! Dal drew back his prosthetic foot and kicked the tire of his truck. He couldn't figure out what was wrong. Why had the vehicle stopped working? Why now? He couldn't even tell where the plume of gray smoke was coming from. An unexplainable breakdown. He'd rebuilt this entire engine himself. He knew every tube and wire in this truck. Yet he didn't know what was wrong and why it had stopped running.

Unless…

No, he didn't believe in God's intervention anymore. Too many bad things had happened to him over the years. But then, the Lord had brought Julie back into his life. A coincidence or providence? She'd been so good for him that he couldn't believe she was anything but a godsend. And he hated himself for breaking her heart.

Doubts assailed his mind. He wasn't going back. He couldn't hurt her again. He couldn't…

"Hey, stranger, do you need a ride?"

Dal whirled around. Julie stood there, her car parked behind his truck. He'd been so engrossed in his problems that he hadn't heard her get out of the car.

"Julie." His voice sounded hoarse to his own ears. He squinted against the bright sunlight, thinking she must be a mirage. A wishful vision of his imagination.

She leaned her hip against his truck and folded her arms. Dressed in her running clothes, she looked slim and beautiful. Sunlight highlighted the streaks of gold in her chestnut hair. She appeared relaxed, but he saw the fire in her eyes and the stubborn lift of her jaw. She was angry. Good and mad.

At him.

He shook his head, not laughing. Wishing she hadn't found him. Thinking he should leave but yearning to stay right here.

With her.

"How…how did you find me?" he asked.

"Cade told me you'd left town." Her bottom lip quivered as though she were biting back tears.

He could read between the lines. He hadn't just left town. He'd left her, too.

Her eyes hardened, the tears dried to a cold, angry blur. "Are you ready to settle down now? Or would you rather just keep on running?"

"No, I don't want to keep running." He refused to look at her, his heart filled with utter desolation. He didn't want to hurt her. He didn't want to leave. And yet, he couldn't stay.

"Then stay." Her words were no more than a whispered plea, carried on the morning breeze.

He met her eyes. "I can't."

"Can't or won't?"

Both! "I want to be fair to you, Jules. To keep you safe."

"So you do that by abandoning me?"

"No. I didn't mean to hurt you."

"Leaving without saying goodbye is a strange way of showing that."

He flinched. "I didn't look at it quite like that."

"Well, I do." She moved in close and lifted her hands to cup his face. Forcing him to look at her. To meet her eyes. Refusing to back down. "Life is unfair, Dal. To everyone. To you and me. But God is the great equalizer. He can make everything right again, if you'll just give Him half a chance. If you'll just give us a chance."

The warmth of her hands seeped into his skin, warming his frozen heart. He'd tried to run away, but he couldn't hide from the Lord. And in that moment, he believed God had sent Julie after him. To bring him home again. "This isn't about you, Jules. It's about me."

"Not anymore. You love me. I know you do, so don't deny it. And I love you. So now it's about us. If you leave me, you'll break my heart. And I don't think you're the kind of man to do that to a woman he loves. Are you?"

"Oh, Jules."

He stepped back and she dropped her hands. But it wasn't enough distance. Even if she lived on the other side of the planet, it would never be far enough away. Not for him.

She was right. He couldn't hurt her. Even if she stopped loving him some day, it'd be his heart that would be broken. And he loved her so much that he'd prefer that over hurting her.

"You remember I told you once that I started running when I was fifteen years old?" she asked.

He nodded, unable to speak.

"Well, it's occurred to me since then that I've been running almost my entire life, Dal. Lately, I've started wondering what I'm running away from. I don't want to run anymore. And I'm wondering what you're running away from, too. I mean, how much do we have to prove to the world before we cut ourselves some slack? Will we ever be good enough for each other?"

"I don't know."

"Your words tell me that you're tired of being alone, just like me."

"Yes." But it might not make a difference. Not for them. Not ever.

"Then don't you think it's time we accept ourselves for who we are and stop running away?" she said.

He lifted one shoulder. "I don't know if that's possible, Jules."

"It is if we decide it is. I want you in my life, Dal. I'm willing to take that step if you are. And I know, with you by my side, I'll be strong enough to face whatever life throws our way. But I'm afraid if you leave me now I'll never recover. I'll never be whole again. Please, Dal. Please don't leave me ever again."

The blood drained from his face and he swallowed hard. Her eyes gleamed with tears, and he realized how much he'd hurt her. How much he never wanted to hurt her again.

Dal looked over Julie's shoulder as another truck pulled up. Cade got out, his expression solemn as he sauntered toward them. And then Dal knew the truth. Cade must have done something to sabotage Dal's truck. To make sure he couldn't go anywhere. To give Julie time to find him.

Dal wanted to be angry at Cade, but he just couldn't. And it occurred to Dal that Cade had done the Lord's work today. Cade had intervened when Dal was about to do something completely stupid.

Like walk away from the woman he loved.

"Well, I can see Cade's here to help you out." Julie bit her bottom lip. "I'm going back to town now. If you want a life with me, you know where to find me. But you'll have to make the next move, Dal. Our happiness is in your hands. And I'm trusting you to do the right thing."

Turning, she walked away, giving a simple, curt nod to Cade as she opened the door to her car and slid inside.

Dal stared after her, his mind filled with a trillion scrambled thoughts. He opened his mouth to call her back, but didn't speak. Deep in his heart, he felt numb and empty. Convinced that his leaving town was the best thing for both of them.

Two hours later, Julie sat on the steps of her front porch. She'd missed the 5K race and hadn't returned to the park to see the winners. Right now, she didn't care. Not when everything of importance had collapsed around her.

Her entire world had left town without her.

Looking up, she saw a truck parked in front of her house. She blinked to clear her eyes, thinking it was identical to the vehicle Dal drove. But it wasn't his. It couldn't be. It…

And then she saw him. Standing beside her mailbox, watching her. A slight smile curved his handsome mouth, his eyes glowing with wonder and love.

She came to her feet so fast that she almost fell headfirst into her flowerbed.

"Hi there," he said.

"Hi," she squeaked.

And then she was in his arms. She didn't know if he ran to her or she ran to him. Maybe they met each other halfway in the middle of the yard. It didn't matter. Not anymore. Not as long as they were together.

"You came back for me," she murmured against the collar of his shirt.

"And I'll never leave you again."

She breathed in his warm, clean scent, hardly able to believe he was really here. "You sure I'm what you want?"

"Oh, yes. I can't even think about living the rest of my life without you in it," he said.

His arms tightened around her and she

burrowed closer. His words filled her to overflowing.

"I love you, Dal. I always have. That was why I fell and sprained my ankle that day I was jogging out in the fields. I saw you and couldn't believe my eyes. I was just so afraid. So afraid you wouldn't want me ever again. I… I'm used merchandise. My foster father took everything I had to give you."

"Don't say that. It's not true." His voice sounded harsh. "I just want you, Jules. That man wasn't a foster dad. He wasn't a father. He was a monster. A beast. I hope he rots in prison for what he did to you."

"It might not be Christian to think that way, but so do I. He needs to stay where he can't hurt other children," Julie said. "But you've made me feel whole again. Like I'm a person of value and that I matter."

"You do, honey. You do to me." He kissed her forehead, her ear, her lips. Quick, furious kisses that left her feeling joyful and breathless.

Her heart did a myriad of somersaults.

Speaking the words out loud, she felt so free. Finally free.

"I love you, Jules. So very much. But those three words don't begin to describe how I feel about you. *I love you* seems so paltry compared to how I really feel about you."

She lifted her face to him, her eyes dripping with tears. "Do you mean that, Dal?"

He gave a hoarse laugh. "Oh, yes. I'm crazy about you, girl."

"And I'm crazy about you." Her voice trembled with the intensity of her emotions.

"Okay, then. Marry me and put me out of my misery. Please, sweetheart."

His words brought a zipping thrill to her chest. "You know, I come with extra baggage."

"Me, too. I'll always have an amputated leg. I'll always walk with a slight limp."

"Oh, I couldn't care less about that. But I'm talking about a child."

He spiked a brow upward. "Huh?"

"Marcus."

"Marcus?" He frowned in confusion.

"I made some inquiries with his social worker. I love that little boy and plan to adopt him. I got word yesterday that they're going to speak with him. If he's in agreement, he's mine. My son. So if you marry me, you get both of us. We're a package deal. Congratulations, Dal. You're about to become a father."

He blinked, and a smile widened his mouth with awe. "Really?"

"Yes, I told you there were ways for us to have a family together. And I meant it."

He threw back his head and laughed. "You never cease to amaze me, Jules. I think that's a wonderful idea. In fact, on the drive over here, I was hoping to ask you about Marcus. He needs a family, and heaven knows we need him, too. We'll be a real family. As long as we're together. Say you'll be mine and make me the happiest man on earth. Please."

"Yes, oh, yes!" Wild laughter shook her chest.

He kissed her. A soft, gentle kiss that filled her soul and kept growing from there. His kiss grew stronger, filled with the passion they'd both kept locked inside their hearts for all these long, lonely years. And then she knew she'd never be alone again. And life seemed wonderful all of a sudden. So grand and filled with marvelous possibilities.

When he drew back and gazed down into her eyes, she saw that he was crying, too.

"I guess we're both finished running," she said.

He gave her a tender smile. "At least from anything other than a marathon. I'm afraid you're stuck with me now."

"Good. That's what I needed to hear."

"As long as we have each other, there's nothing we can't do. Even have more children someday."

"Yes, together." And she believed every single word.

Epilogue

Five years later, the scrumptious aroma of baking filled the kitchen. The last batch of chocolate-chip cookies had just gone into the oven. Julie set the timer for ten minutes, then reached for the empty mixing bowl and submerged it into the sink of hot, sudsy water. Her round tummy bumped against the counter and she paused, feeling the thumping movements of her and Dal's baby inside her. This would be their third child.

Correction. Their fifth. First, they'd married and adopted Marcus. Then Teddy, who was now eight years old and had freckles and red hair the color of a new fire engine.

Then Julie had discovered she was pregnant, and they'd had twin girls eighteen months earlier. Now Julie was five months along with this new baby.

Another boy.

Clasping the dishcloth in her hand, she scrubbed cookie dough off the bowl, rinsed it and set it aside in the dish rack. As she worked, she hummed a lullaby to herself. A song she remembered her own mother singing to her when she'd been young. Julie marveled at the miracle God had worked for her and Dal, feeling more content than ever before in her life. Who would have believed that just five years earlier, neither she nor Dal had thought they could ever have kids. And here they were expecting their fifth child!

A thump came from the back of the house. Dal and the kids must be finished raking the fall leaves out of the backyard.

Her husband and their children.

"Here comes the Tickle Monster." Dal's happy voice boomed throughout the house.

A cacophony of delighted squeals erupted down the hallway. Dal thundered into the kitchen, holding a twin girl in each of his arms. Marcus clung to Dal's back, laughing at the top of his lungs. Teddy's C-Leg prosthesis caused little hindrance as he bear-hugged Dal's waist. The man looked like a giant spider with so many kids hanging off his tall frame. The border collie they'd brought home from the animal shelter ten months earlier jumped up and barked, scrambling around the melee of boisterous kids.

Jerking her head around, Julie gazed at her husband and children with amusement. As usual, bedlam had exploded in their house. With this many kids, they were never a quiet family. And she loved it. The caring. The camaraderie. She'd never be alone again.

"Mom!" Teddy ran to her, throwing his arms around her thick waist.

She picked him up, holding him to the side of her baby bump. She looked him in the eyes and kissed the tip of his nose. "Hi, sweetheart. Have you been having fun?"

He nodded. "Yeah. We jumped in the leaves."

"Well, I hope after you were finished, you bagged them up for the garbageman to haul off."

The boy rested a hand on her shoulder, his innocent face carved in a serious expression as he offered reassurance. It made him look so much like his father that it made her throat ache. "Don't worry, Mom. We took care of it. It's all cleaned up."

"Cookies! Thanks, Mom," Marcus exclaimed.

He dropped away from his dad's back and snatched a warm morsel off the cooling rack Julie had laid out on the table.

She gave Dal a dubious glance, noticing a dried leaf clinging to his dark hair. "I can see you've got the kids all wound up tighter than springs. Thank goodness you got some work done, too."

Dal flashed a wide grin, a laugh rumbling

inside his chest. "Yes, ma'am. The leaves are all raked and bagged up for the garbageman."

"Mom, we played hide-and-seek, too, and I hid in the leaves," Marcus said.

Wiping her left hand on a dish towel, she reached for each of her boys to give them a kiss and a tight squeeze. "You did, huh? Is that why it took you all so long?"

"Yeah, but it's Dad's fault. He brought out the Tickle Monster." Teddy showed a toothless smile as he spoke around a mouthful of cookie.

Julie chuckled, washing the beaters while she listened to her children tell her how the Tickle Monster had kept throwing them into the leaves and prevented them from getting their work done. Of course, Dal was the Tickle Monster. If she weren't so far along in her pregnancy, she would have been outside with them, jumping in the leaves herself. It felt so good to know her children were happy. To know they all belonged to one another. A real family for keeps.

To add to the joyful chaos, the phone

started ringing. Julie glanced at the wall, feeling a bit flustered with her hands immersed in a sink full of water. She snatched a dishcloth to dry them off, but Dal beat her to the phone.

Planting a quick kiss on her lips, he reached for the handset. "I've got it, hon. You kids, pipe down for just a few minutes."

He handed one of the twins off to Marcus, and the children quieted to a dull roar.

"Hush, Barkley." Teddy latched on to the dog's collar to calm the agitated mutt.

"Hello." Dal looked at Julie and smiled, waggling his eyebrows at her. He swept little Deanne up against his shoulder and gazed into her large brown eyes as he held the phone against his ear. She promptly tried to stick her fingers into his mouth, and he pressed his lips tightly together.

Julie couldn't suppress a delighted laugh. With a busy career and a houseful of kids, she figured Saturday mornings would never be tranquil again. Thank goodness Dal was such a hands-on father, and his work at the horse camp allowed him to shuttle their children around. During the winter months when he wasn't so busy working at Sunrise Ranch, he was able to do the bulk of the laundry. Without his generous assistance, she didn't know how she could do it all. Of course, a kind child-care provider helped out with the younger children, as well. And during the summer months, Marcus and Teddy shadowed Dal at the horse camp to help with the amputee kids. Life wasn't calm and serene around their house the rest of the week, either. And she wouldn't have it any other way.

"Trisha. Hi! How are you doing?" Dal paused for a moment, listening. "We're all fine. Julie's feeling good with this new pregnancy. It hasn't been as difficult as it was with the twins."

Julie's ears perked up when she heard Trisha's name. The only Trisha she knew was the social worker who had helped them adopt both Marcus and Teddy. Life had thrown them some surprises, but Julie remembered a time when she had no family at all. She figured it just couldn't get better than this. Taking a deep inhale, she savored these precious moments with her little ones.

She rinsed a dish and set it in the dish rack, eavesdropping on Dal's end of the conversation. The boys took the twins over to the table where they sat and munched on cookies. While Dal continued his conversation, Julie dried her hands and poured milk for each child. She put a sippy lid on the cups for the little girls, who were more prone to spills.

"You have one more child for us?"

Julie straightened quickly and spun around, pressing a hand across her middle.

Dal met her wide gaze across the room. "Yes, Julie's right here with me. She's listening."

Another long pause.

"Her name is Melanie, and she's missing her right arm at the shoulder? An orphan. No parents to love her. Almost six years old. A real sweetie. Long blond hair and blue eyes."

He repeated the conversation out loud for Julie's benefit. When she thought about this little girl needing a family, her heart gave a powerful squeeze. Another amputee child without parents needed a loving home. A feeling of anticipation grew within Julie, along with a fear that she wouldn't be strong enough to care for another child. And yet, God had strengthened her to meet the needs of her quickly growing family. She couldn't believe how fast time had passed. And she remembered something her own mother had told her once, so very long ago.

Hands full now, hearts full later.

Yes, that described Julie's feelings perfectly. She was busy. But one day, her children would be grown and she'd have them forever. So much joy that she could hardly contain it within her heart.

"You're looking for a home for her, huh? Another adoption," Dal said.

No big surprise there. Trisha only called when she wanted to check up on the kids. Or to see if they were interested in adopting another child into their home.

Julie looked around her kitchen, filled to overflowing with kids, warmth and love.

Her gaze locked with Dal's, and she saw the adoration and happiness shining in his eyes. Without saying anything, each knew how the other one felt. For a couple who had believed they would never marry and have the blessing of children in their lives, their house was now full. The home they'd bought together wasn't overly large, but it was comfortable, clean and warm. Their kitchen was filled with good, nutritious food. The minivan parked out front included room for eight seats. And it looked as though they'd need it.

Their choices might seem strange to someone else. Too many kids. Too much work. Someone who didn't understand where they'd been and how much they cherished their family might not approve. But that didn't matter to them. Julie had nothing to prove to anyone. Not anymore. The Lord had wrought a miracle in their lives. For her and Dal. For their family. They had each other. They had everything. Their whole world was right here, within their small home. What more could Julie ask for?

Lifting her head, her eyes burned with

tears of gratitude. Dal paused, patiently awaiting her answer. She walked to him, and he opened one arm for her to snuggle close against his side. She knew without a doubt that he'd tell Trisha no if she didn't feel good about it. Dal's loving consideration for her well-being touched Julie's heart as nothing else could. For him, Julie and the kids always came first, before his own wants and needs. And she tried to do the same for him. They had each other's backs, keeping God at the center of their union. Putting their marriage and family above all other pursuits.

Gazing up into her husband's eyes, Julie nodded and Dal gave a short laugh of happiness. And as he said the buoyant words into the handset, Julie knew it was the right decision for them to make.

"Yes, we have room for one more."

* * * * *

Dear Reader,

We each have infirmities of body and spirit. Life is so hard. It is a proving ground for us to learn to live by faith and to keep God's commandments. The Lord has provided us with scriptures to help show us the way we should live. And yet, when we are in the depths of our despair, it can still be so difficult.

In *The Forest Ranger's Return,* both the hero and heroine struggle with their own infirmities. Physical and mental ailments can diminish our self-worth and cause us to doubt ourselves. But we understand from the scriptures that Christ knows each and every one of us personally. He knows our loneliness and difficulties. The atonement of Jesus Christ envelops all of the trials and adversity that any of us will encounter in this life. The worth of a soul is so great in the eyes of God. We are His children. And He loves us unconditionally, in spite of our physical and mental limitations.

I hope you enjoy reading *The Forest Ranger's Return,* and I invite you to visit my website at www.leighbale.com to learn more about my books.

May you find peace in the Lord's words!
Leigh Bale

Questions for Discussion

1. In *The Forest Ranger's Return,* Julie Granger is a forest ranger who lost her parents when she was a teenager. She ended up being put into foster care and yanked out of the happy life she'd known with her boyfriend, Dal Savatch. Have you or someone you know been raised in foster care? Was it a good experience? Why or why not?

2. Dallin Savatch is a U.S. Marine who lost one of his legs while saving the life of his best friend, who was a prisoner of war. Dal was able to cope with losing his leg, but his fiancée turned her back on him when she found out he might not be able to father a child because of his injuries. Do you think Dal's fiancée was wise to walk away from him the way she did? Why or why not?

3. Because of the abuse she endured as an orphaned teenager, Julie wondered nu-

merous times if God had abandoned her. Do you believe He did? Why or why not?

4. Unlike Julie, Dal never felt that God had abandoned him, even after Dal lost his leg in the war. Why do you think some people feel forsaken by God while others do not? Have you or someone you care about ever felt rejected by the Lord?

5. We each have our own free agency to choose how we will react to the hardships of life. Why do you think God allows bad things to happen to good people? Likewise, why do you think good things happen to bad people? Can we pray away someone else's free agency to choose what they will think, feel and do in this life? Why or why not?

6. Marcus is a ten-year-old boy who lost his left hand in a plane crash that killed both of his parents. He was angry at everyone until Julie told him that his parents' death was not his fault. Why do

you think Julie's talk with Marcus had such a great impact on him? Have you ever blamed yourself for something you had no control over? If you were able to overcome that problem, what did it finally take for you to let go of your guilt?

7. Because he may not have been able to father a child, Dal continued to fight his attraction to Julie. If they were to marry, he feared Julie might come to hate him later on. Do you think Dal was wise in his decision? Why or why not?

8. Loneliness had become a constant companion for Dal and Julie. Many people are alone, but they still lead happy, fulfilled lives. Have you or someone you know ever lived in a constant state of loneliness? How did they find joy in life? How can prayer and faith in God help us overcome our loneliness?

9. Julie was sexually abused by one of her foster fathers. Because she felt unworthy and embarrassed, she cut off all ties

with Dal and determined that she could never marry. Do you think she made the right decision? Why or why not? How do you think our nation's legal system should handle pedophiles? Why?

10. Julie was a forest ranger who must keep the laws when it came to altering a trail or campsite. During the open meeting to discuss Dal's proposed changes to Gilway Trail, Julie took a lot of verbal abuse from one of the ranchers who did not want the amputee kids from Sunrise Ranch to use the trail. What might you have said to this rancher? If you had been Dal, what might you have done? Why?

11. Even though she already had a very busy job, Julie felt drawn to the amputee kids and loved her volunteer work at Sunrise Ranch. Have you ever volunteered to serve others? Did you have a positive experience with your ser-

vice? What made it positive or negative for you? Why?

12. When Dal introduced the amputee kids at Sunrise Ranch to Polly, the little mare with a prosthetic leg, he told them that there was nothing they couldn't do if they wanted it badly enough to find a way to make it happen. Do you think Dal's encouragement was realistic, or did it give the kids false hope? Why or why not?

13. Neither Julie nor Dal thought they'd ever marry, let alone raise six children together. Some people believe this is too many children for one couple to raise, even if they can provide a stable, loving home. Do you agree? Why?

14. One of Dal's friends who lost his limbs in the war commits suicide after his wife divorces him. Unfortunately, this is a very real situation today. Many of our armed forces are coming home seriously wounded, either from physical in-

juries or post-traumatic stress disorder. Some of them can't cope anymore and take their own lives. How do you think our Heavenly Father feels about these precious souls?

15. After Dal left town, Julie went after him. When she found him, she disclosed her love for him and asked him to stay. Knowing what Julie had been through in her life, do you think she was wise to leave Dal to make up his own mind? If he hadn't returned home and come to propose marriage to her, what do you think Julie should have done? Should she have gone after Dal again and again or finally let him go? Why?